DROWNING In Your SLEEP

Donna Galloway

FriesenPress

One Printers Way
Altona, MB R0G 0B0
Canada

www.friesenpress.com

Copyright © 2024 by Donna Galloway
First Edition — 2024

All rights reserved.

No part of this publication may be reproduced in any form, or by any means, electronic or mechanical, including photocopying, recording, or any information browsing, storage, or retrieval system, without permission in writing from FriesenPress.

ISBN
978-1-03-832110-7 (Hardcover)
978-1-03-832109-1 (Paperback)
978-1-03-832111-4 (eBook)

1. FICTION, MYSTERY & DETECTIVE

Distributed to the trade by The Ingram Book Company

Best Wishes Larissa.

Donna Galloway

DROWNING IN YOUR SLEEP

WINNIPEG, MANITOBA, CANADA, 2024

To the memory of Gerhard Schilke, who said,

"Little girl, you can do or be anything you want in life…"

So, she wrote it down.

This is a book of fiction. It is a work of cognitive behavioral therapy, written over a period of twenty-two years. Any references to historical events, real people, real places, or real things are used fictitiously. Other names, characters, places, and events are products of the author's imagination. Any resemblance to actual events, places, products, or persons, living or dead, is entirely coincidental.

INTRODUCTION

Night terrors, *pavor nocturnus*, the things that go bump in the night. I have carried the torture with me for more than fifty years. Cognitive behavior therapy, meditation, and medication have helped greatly with clinical depression and major anxiety, but I long to sleep peacefully. I am often riddled with fear; it is a part of my daily life. I wake up screaming, sweating, crying, and struggling for breath.

PTSD. The monsters come in many forms. Sometimes, in a single dream, I may be trying to save someone from a brutal death or trying to get away from it myself. Sometimes, I am trapped, running in slow motion while the beasts devour my flesh. One ongoing terror I still have starts with two grizzly bears tearing every piece of tissue from my body. I hang upside down over a picnic table while they fight over which limb to tear into first. They start with my head. It is the same dream over and over. All these years, they have never finished their feast. And then there are the times I dream long, brutally explicit tales like the one you are about to read, hitting me in elaborate waves of terror, the experience so horrifying, my heart feels like it will pound out of my chest in response. I desperately want it to stop, but of course, it does not. It is not until I feel I may die from the fright that finally the grace of God wakes me.

My husband throws his arms around me and assures me the extremely detailed horror, of which only movies should be made, is not real, even though I have just lived through it—again. I am safe at home in my bed, he tells me. I am okay. All is well. I swing my legs over the side as I catch my breath and put my feet on the floor, just to be sure he is telling the truth.

And then I turn to my journal and write, to get this out of my head, out of my subconscious, wondering if it will help. The story you are about to read is a detailed night terror I experienced that evolved over time, in torturous pieces, with characters and personalities that developed from simple to complex, giving off lightning-bolt energy, haunting me so much that it took more than twenty years to write. It almost scared me to death.

Donna Galloway

PROLOGUE

THE YEAR: 2031. The crime rate in Washington, D.C., is rampant. You cannot go anywhere without having your picture taken. Building corners, traffic lights, public parks, every bank, high-rise, street corner, restaurant, and bar will light you up. In fact, the widespread presence of cameras is so prevalent that it's become impossible to monitor them all and their grainy outputs have become harder to read.

All seven districts have their own chief of police, and there are more undercover detectives than ever before. There is going to be a murder. There are going to be several.

Now heed this warning: Ladies, if you meet a stranger on the street who asks you out for a drink, or wants to buy you a cup of coffee, take a walk in the park, or have a quiet lunch, don't go with him. Don't even give them the time of day. Don't stop to help him. Don't look into his eyes. Run. Don't walk.

This man is captivating. He is charming. And he's a serial killer with a keen appetite. A seasoned detective is on the case. Unfortunately, the only way to catch this killer … is to die.

CHAPTER 1

WASHINGTON, D.C.

DETECTIVE JACK FAVRO smashed the top of his alarm clock with such force it broke into several pieces. Of course, this is certain to happen when you use the handle of your gun to hit the snooze button. His Glock 22 had so many dings in it, it looked like he'd bought it off the street. But it was definitely police issue.

Another day, another hangover. It was 5:22 a.m. *Gonna need another clock*, he thought. Favro felt like he'd been kicked several times in the stomach. But there were no bruises. It would have made a great story down at the station if it had been some smart-mouthed drug dealer he'd been trying to arrest. But unfortunately, this Tennessee fellow came from a bottle. Favro's head was pounding. His eyes were burning. Hell, even his teeth hurt.

He raised his hands in the air. "Ohhh … No, thank you. No coffee for me," he mumbled to himself on the way to the bathroom, stumbling over the bottle he'd emptied just a few hours earlier.

Favro's aching thirty-eight-year-old body hit the shower, and then hit the streets, unshaven as usual. He didn't know it yet, but it was going to be a long day. A very long day.

When he rolled into the station just after six a.m., all eyes were on him. Before the crew stood the epitome of an undercover cop, with one bonus: He was hot! He had a swagger. With faded blue jeans, a black leather jacket covering a rugged muscular build, a day-old beard, and black wavy hair, this was no get-up. This was Jack Favro. He was a joy to few, and a pain in the ass to most.

He plunked himself down in a chair in front of Pattie's desk. She was an unpretentious brunette with impossibly long eyelashes, framing the doe eyes that focused only on him—always on him. They were the same age; however, Favro's hard living gave him a rough appeal. And even though the sometimes-appalling rumors about him were true, he was still extremely alluring.

Pattie, with excellent posture and her long hair up in a tight bun, was very good at her job despite the distraction of Jack Favro. She was Chief Paul Beckwith's assistant and had been for twelve years. She was also the one person in Favro's life who brought him genuine joy. He loved the banter between them, the back-and-forth sarcasm. Her desk always served as somewhat of a barrier. She couldn't detect liquor on his breath—or so he thought.

"What's up for today, duckling?" he asked with the charismatic twist he saved only for her.

"That's not funny! Where have you been all night? He's been texting and calling you," she tried to whisper.

"Why?"

"They have another letter!"

Favro stood slowly and squared his shoulders. He could feel the hair on the back of his neck stand at attention. Curiosity and paranoia had their ugly hands clenched around his throat. His fist went to his mouth as he coughed and made a beeline for the coffee machine about ten feet from her desk.

A quick peek through the glass windows of Chief Beckwith's office found the two of them staring straight at each other.

"Has it been processed yet?"

Pattie looked up at him. "He's waiting for you, Fav. This one is different from the others."

The chief had a look on his face that meant serious business. He'd seen it before. Either something was very wrong, or he was in deep shit—or both. Favro was not a "by the book" type cop. He often did things wrong, and he often got into trouble. But he solved more cases with his unconventional methods than most, so his techniques and procedures were often overlooked. But sometimes they weren't. It depended on how much the damages cost and whether the chief had been humiliated.

Hoping the coffee would hide the whiskey, he took a hot sip, and then another.

The chief's door was booted open, and Beckwith yelled out from his chair, "Favro, you get your ass in here!"

He turned towards Pattie. "Why is this one different?"

She whispered, "It's addressed to you."

Oh no, Favro thought. *Here we go.*

He entered the office where Chief Beckwith was fuming and supporting himself on his desk with white knuckles.

"GPS says you've been home all night," he seethed. "Do you know how many times I've called and how many texts I've sent you? You have to turn that device on for it to work, you know."

"It's on vibrate … in the kitchen."

"What the hell for?"

"It has a tendency to ring."

"Oh … Oh my God, is today smartass day? Sit! Down!"

Favro made a mental note: *Tone it down*. Beckwith handed him a manila file folder.

"Our serial killer is active again. We found the body last night. And there's a letter here addressed to you with all the clues! I don't know why it's addressed to you, but we might have received it earlier if you checked your fucking mail slot once in a while! It doesn't help us now! And why would he do that? Why would he suddenly send the letter just to you?"

Favro's thoughts were moving at the speed of light.

Looks like I'm going to have to spill the beans.

Favro knew a lot about this killer, just not enough to catch him. He knew that Washington, D.C., was his playground, and that he was a ruthless player. That each murder site left nothing to the imagination, and that each one was becoming more graphic and violent than the last. These weren't kidnappings. This murderer never asked for money. He would send letters to the station indicating that he was going to "work" again, along with clues to the "jobsite," and then kill his victim immediately.

The police were hunting a serial killer and searching for dead bodies, though there had never been enough time between receiving the letters and the killings to save the victim. They needed to be master detectives. Favro's job was to figure out why this killer was killing and find him before the next letter arrived.

He ran his fingers through his wavy hair, still damp from the shower that had revived him.

"Two Massachusetts Ave. NE," he said.

"What did you say?" the chief demanded. You could blow the smoke off the top of his head. He was fuming.

Favro already had a copy of the letter because it had been sent to his home address three weeks ago. He didn't have to read the report. He knew exactly where they'd found the body.

That was the message the killer had sent. It was the game he refused to stop playing, and that he had chosen *him* to play with. That's what bothered Favro. That's what pissed him off.

Without looking any further, he tossed the manila folder back onto the chief's desk. "National Postal Museum."

"You wanna tell me how the fuck you know that? Because that report hasn't left this office. I shut it down last night. The scene, the investigator—who was supposed to be you by the way—the medical examiner, the photos, everything. Shut it down!"

Well, Favro did tell the chief "how the fuck" he'd known that, and a whole lot more. When he was finished, he was certain Chief Beckwith was going to have a coronary.

In his last letter, one of the clues had been a vintage five-cent stamp depicting Benjamin Franklin. The body was found wrapped up like a parcel waiting to be mailed. It had the exact amount of postage for her weight, stuck all over her body. She had been dead about a week, strapped to the top of the stagecoach display in the National Postage Museum. She wasn't noticed until the body had started to stink. The frustrating part was that although Favro had had all the clues, he just hadn't been able to find her fast enough. The girl hadn't stood a chance.

"Pattie told me this letter is different from the others."

Beckwith stared straight at him. "Yes, you moron. That's why I've been trying to reach you," he said, holding up the letter from Favro's mail slot. "He only wants to play with you!"

The chief had no idea that they'd been "playing" together from the beginning. The first two murders had been a total embarrassment to Beckwith. And now this one. The mayor was going to roast him. Favro had done his due diligence, but this serial killer had left nothing behind they could use to find him. No DNA on file. No fingerprints in AFIS. And only grainy images were captured on cameras, meaning they couldn't use facial recognition. He was going to have to use one of his unconventional tactics.

The chief is gonna freak.

CHAPTER 2

STONEBROOK PENITENTIARY

WARDEN HENDERSON PUSHED his chair back so hard, it toppled over.

"What do you mean you're not gonna be finished on schedule? This isn't about the damned contract anymore, Jenkins! Which, I might add, you and those idiots you employ breached two months after you started this damn project! I've got a prisoner who is supposed to go swimming in two weeks, and God damn it, he will swim even if I gotta take him to your house and use your bloody Jacuzzi! Have I made myself clear, Mr. Jenkins?"

"Yes, sir."

Jenkins closed the office door quietly behind him. He knew the routine by now. He'd been in this office three times for tongue lashings.

Before Henderson could page his secretary, she was at his door with a glass of water and some seltzer.

"Alice! Get me Professor Collier on the line. I need some reassurance that this tank is gonna do what it's supposed to do when they finally finish the bloody thing."

Alice picked his chair back up, then straightened the papers on his desk. Looking once over her shoulder, she then closed the office door on her way out. She'd worked with the warden for fourteen years and knew the routine as well. She'd been fifteen minutes late for work last month and had paid for it for three days. Everybody suffered when the warden wasn't happy. And clearly, he wasn't happy.

Henderson crossed his arms and stared glumly out his window. The cold concrete yard was such a hard contrast to the green grass that sprouted up just outside the fence-line. Right after four in the afternoon, the sun would hit the only visible cherry tree. He could barely see it by the time he left the penitentiary at five, so he made a point of being at the window at this time every day to see it. Never showing his true feelings to anyone, sometimes he felt like a prisoner himself. Everything he wanted was always beyond his reach. He was never satisfied. Looking at that little cherry tree each day before he left calmed his nerves. But he would never tell a soul. People might think he was actually happy once in a while. He couldn't have that going on.

Jenkins's Masonry & Construction Company had to have the new wing at Stonebrook completed before the mayor's tour, and it was going to house a remarkable new invention. It had to go without a hitch. If things weren't absolutely perfect, it wouldn't be Professor Collier who took the heat. It wouldn't be Jenkins and his band of flunkies who went down. It would be the warden who got crucified. It was always the warden when it came to penitentiaries, and Henderson couldn't afford a screw up. His temper had reared its ugly head in past ventures, and the mayor had ended up with egg on his face.

I need this project, he thought. *It's time to make a name for myself.*

He needed it to go well.

Professor Russell Collier slowly set his tablet back on his desk. He didn't like threats. He had been working day and night for the past twelve years on this project, perfecting what he was certain would be the greatest achievement by a scientific engineer this century.

"I am the one who came up with the theory! I am the one who engineered this work! This masterpiece! I don't need some dumbass warden telling me, 'You better know what you're doing!'" he mimicked sarcastically.

Collier's face was turning red now. The warden hadn't come down once to tour the end results—to see how well he had succeeded. He smashed his tablet to the floor and crushed it with his foot. "To hell with the deadline; it's ready now," he hissed.

Composed, Professor Collier stood up. With his arms crossed, he stared into the future: The Narcoleptic Sleep Tank.

The slow-moving water inside the massive tank was so calming, it was almost hypnotic. Standing in the shadows of the dimly lit room, one would barely notice the baboon, floating lifeless at the top of the tank.

A slow smile crept over his face. *Yes,* he thought, *the mayor will surely be pleased.*

FEDERAL COURTHOUSE
333 Constitution Ave. NW

THE HONORABLE Carol Mason of the U.S. District Court for the District of Columbia sat quietly in her chambers. *It's too* *hot to be wearing this robe,* she thought, *and why does it have to be black? Yes, honor, dignity, wisdom, and justice, blah blah blah. Couldn't it be white? No, that wouldn't work because judges rarely deliver good news, so let's dress us in black and make us the bad guys everyone thinks we are anyway ... Whew! This is an historical day.* She was feeling the pressure.

Delivering Edgar Sanderson's sentence for murder in the second degree of six-year-old Audrey Madison, and at the same time being the first person to formally present to the world and crowded courtroom the first sentence with a brand-new invention was a lot of pressure. It was a new invention that people had thought would never come to fruition. They had heard bits and pieces but had no idea it was real, and they also had no idea how critical it was. A development so critical, it would affect not only the lives of prisoners and their families but many working within the judicial system as well. It would affect the national economy. Many jobs would be influenced. Some people were going to be confused. Some were going to be shocked. One thing was for sure: There was going to be disorder. *God, I hate it when there's disorder,* she thought.

As Judge Mason entered the courtroom, everyone stood.

"This is case number 41370, United States versus Edgar William Sanderson," the bailiff announced. "This court will come to order. Please be seated."

The bailiff handed papers to the judge, and then dutifully stepped back into his position to the left side of her bench. The judge looked towards Audrey's family, holding their gaze for a moment. She then scanned the courtroom and its crowded gallery.

Here we go, she thought.

"Good morning, ladies and gentlemen. Before I begin ... I will not tolerate any outbursts or hysteria of any kind in my courtroom today. Any such disturbances will result in immediate removal of such person or persons."

The nervous fidgeting of the crowd gathered to watch in the court's gallery came to a halt. They sat silently; all eyes fixed on the proceedings. The trial had been exceptionally hard on the little girl's family, and the entire nation wanted Sanderson's head on a platter.

The judge scanned the crowd again. They seemed to salivate before her. She wondered if what she was about to deliver would be enough to feed all these hungry lions.

She continued. "The immediate family will be allowed into my chambers following these proceedings. I will answer any questions they may have at that time.

"Let's begin. Edgar Sanderson, please stand and face this court."

He was ashen gray. But for his orange prison clothes, the convict looked homeless. The small amount of hair on his head was greasy, and his nose looked like it had been broken many times. Sanderson's feet and hands were shackled. He had to be helped up, and the ominous sound of the irons echoed throughout the gallery. He was so skinny, the irons pulled him down like weights under water. The two guards had to hold him up. Judge Mason gave him a mere moment to compose himself.

"Mr. Sanderson, you have been found guilty by a jury of your peers of murder in the second degree, in the rape, strangulation, and consequential death of six-year-old Audrey Germaine Madison. The jury was unanimous on this vote, and each member has been individually polled. I have heard your allocution, August 23, 2031, that resulted in said death. On a personal note, I find it disturbing and morally disgusting that you ask no forgiveness and show no remorse for your actions.

"This court hereby sentences you to no less and no more than ten years in a Narcoleptic Sleep Chamber, time to be served in the Stonebrook Penitentiary of Washington, D.C. You are hereby remanded to the custody of the District of Columbia until you can carry out your sentence in the Narcoleptic Sleep Tank."

At that moment, Judge Mason wondered how many people had noticed how she'd worded this, saying, *"you can carry out your sentence"* instead of *"sentence can be carried out."*

Her gavel pounded only once but sounded like thunder on the eardrums of those who sat so silently in the courtroom. Shock and astonishment covered their faces. Everyone was thinking the same thing: *Only ten years? And what is this "Narcoleptic Sleep Chamber?!"* People were pushing and shoving in the courtroom. Voices were being raised. Judge Mason was losing control of her hungry lions.

Sanderson started to sweat profusely. Ten years was not an adequate sentence to this crowded courtroom, but to him, it was a life sentence. Edgar knew exactly what was in store for him. His defense attorney had prepared him for the worst, but his knees felt weak, and as the room began to spin, he heaved his breakfast onto the defense table in front of him. The vile smell and mess dripped down onto the beautiful court seal embedded in the carpet.

The two guards, surprised by this display, released their hold, letting him slip to the ground. On his way down, he smashed his face on the table—another broken nose for Edgar.

Despite the judge's warning, the courtroom was in full discord and disbelief. Guards removed Edgar immediately, and Judge Mason's gavel pounded to no avail. The court cameras continued to roll as the entire nation—and most of the world—watched on. The judge cleared the court for a ten-minute recess. Several warnings and the removal of seven people later, Judge Mason continued the proceedings.

"The introduction of the Narcoleptic Sleep Tank and Storage Chambers is new to our penitentiaries and revolutionary to the justice system as we once knew it. U.S. courts are frequently criticized for being too lenient on criminals. An in-depth look at the justice system and probes of sentences for violent crimes has stirred much controversy.

"The space required to house criminals has become so phenomenal, and the cost so devastating, that many violent offenders are being released before sentences have been completed, and in many cases, even before their eligibility of parole. The crime rates have risen to an all-time high."

Judge Mason then asked that everyone listen carefully as she explained the invention designed specifically to rectify this predicament:

"This new invention, The Narcoleptic Sleep Tank, and its Chambers, is the life work of Professor Russell Collier. The tank itself is a cube, fifteen feet high, fifteen feet wide, and fifteen feet deep. This tank is filled to the top with clear, pure water. And the walls are made of six-inch-thick, shatter-proof glass.

"The offender will be stripped naked and forced down a chute directly into the tank. They are naked because we don't want them to accidentally become entwined in their own clothing. They will not be wearing any face gear, nor will oxygen be provided to them in any way. On the inside of the tank, there will be a large, black, pushdown-style button. It will be clearly marked and visible.

"This button serves one purpose: The prisoners themselves must push this button to initiate injection into the water of the exact quantity for body weight of Sodium Narcoleptic Pentothal. Within eight seconds, the body will be totally paralyzed, without drowning, and be put into a sleep mode. Once the body is determined to be in this mode, it is transferred to a 'Sleep Chamber' for the duration of the sentence.

"Ladies and gentlemen, I would be remiss if I didn't tell you that drowning in the tank is a distinct possibility. If for reasons known only to the offenders, they do not push the sleep-mode button, they will simply succumb to the intake of water and drown. But this is a decision they make themselves; it is entirely up to them.

"Now, let me address an important issue. I am sure many of you sitting in this courtroom today, and watching from across the nation, feel that 'snoozing away' your ten-year sentence is a cakewalk. Well, I'm here to tell you, ladies and gentlemen, it is nothing of the sort. The body will be totally immobilized, and albeit at a much slower pace, it will continue to age in the sleep chamber.

"Also, as an added bonus, as they sleep, they will experience *pavor nocturnus,* otherwise known as Sleep Terror Disorder. The brain will be kept in a constant state of slumber during the deepest stage of NREM sleep. They will have dreams—hideous, vile dreams—and they will have many of them. These horrors will grab hold of their subconscious. They may feel like they're watching sadistic thrillers play over and over in their head, or drowning slowly, with no air to save them, or being chased by the same monsters that chased them when they were little ... This is their punishment. Ten years of unspeakable night terrors—to some, a punishment far worse than death.

"Mr. Sanderson won't have a job when he wakes up. He won't be placed in a halfway house. The only physiotherapy he will receive will be to recover lost muscle mass via electrodes on his legs, beginning three months prior to the termination of his sentence. This is not a kind gesture on our part. It is so that he might stand to walk himself out the front door.

"We are not completely ignorant as to the likely condition of the prisoner's mental health once they are discharged. And as such, each and every prisoner, upon their release date, will be registered for psychoanalysis and ongoing health care, should they choose it. We'll do everything we can to help them from reoffending. However, should they turn these options down, the following measures will take place instead:

"He will not be reunited with his family. If nobody retrieves him upon discharge, he is on his own. He will be monitored by a control tag on his ankle for two years after release, and if he so much as gets a speeding ticket, he goes on a strict probation for a possible re-entry into the tank. We can't do everything for them."

Judge Mason closed the folder in front of her and intertwined her fingers under her chin. Her eyes slowly scanned the courtroom.

"I suspect, upon hearing his sentence, Mr. Sanderson was ill of stomach today because he knows exactly what the future holds for him. In comparison to other penitentiaries, he will not be spending his time playing cards, streaming channels, and smoking in the yard with his new buddies. And he certainly won't be keeping up with current events.

"You see, ladies and gentlemen, as he will continue to age, so will his family and friends. So will society.

"To the Madison family, I do not suggest that anything could possibly console you at this time, but the terrors Edgar Sanderson will experience are horrific. So, you see, this sentence truly will be, in every sense of the word, a nightmare.

"This brings me now to why we have a second option in the tank: Three feet from the black button is an identical red button. Should the offender decide that he cannot or will not withstand the ten-year sentence in the sleep chamber, he will press the black button first, and then the red button immediately after. This action sets off a chain reaction of two chemicals that, when mixed together, will euthanize the convict within eight seconds of initiating the sequence. There is no margin for error here. Should the offender become confused and hit the red button alone, nothing will happen. If the red button is hit before the black, nothing will happen.

"It must be black and then red for euthanasia to be initiated, or just black for sleep mode. A conscious decision must be made by the offender alone to initiate this sequence. Once again, I remind you, if our prisoners do nothing when they get into the tank, they will simply succumb to the intake of water and drown. Not a desirable way to die, but nonetheless, it is a choice they make themselves.

"The sleep chamber that will house the body is a stackable unit and does nothing more than sustain the life of the criminal at minimal cost. These chambers are monitored by computer and very little manpower will be needed; we are fairly certain there aren't going to be any riots in a prison full of sleeping inmates. There is no order to sustain life should prisoners succumb to anything during their sentence. All inmates sign a DNR. Once the chamber is sealed, the prisoner will not be awakened for ten years under any circumstance, including family emergencies, unless of course the unit malfunctions, which is not likely to happen. They are manufactured and monitored exceptionally well.

"There are more than a thousand sleep chambers already built and more coming off the assembly lines as we speak. The penitentiary at Stonebrook houses just over twelve hundred men and approximately seven hundred women. The new wing has an enormous capacity. We won't be running out of room anytime soon. More details will be released to the press, as well as a statement this afternoon by POTUS. The future is here, ladies and gentlemen, and I have concluded my comments for the day. This court is adjourned."

As if in slow motion, the gavel pounded once. Judge Mason rose and descended into her chambers. Silent for only a moment, the wide-eyed, open-mouthed crowd broke into a frenzy of questions that would not be answered until the president's press conference later that day. The frenzy carried out into the streets. It was a good thing they had planned for crowd control. They needed it well into the night.

CHAPTER 3

THE NEXT MORNING back at the station, Favro rolled in at his usual time: late.

"Check these, Pattie," he said, shoving a piece of paper toward her.

"Favro, how many years have you known me?"

"Hmm … Long time."

"Nine! Nine years I've known you, and I'm probably the only woman in your life. Why can't you say those three words I want to hear, just once?"

"Good morning, Pattie?" He scrunched his brow.

"Shut up and give me the paper," she said. "You know I wouldn't have to do this if you had a proper computer in that relic you call a vehicle."

"Heeey! Don't talk about my baby like that!"

She smiled and shook her head.

"Besides, when would we chat?" He loved pushing her buttons.

She wished he would ask her for something else. The chief's door swung open. "All right," she said to him, glancing back at the door, "but this time you owe me."

"Favro! When the two of you have finished your little tea party, I want to see you in my office!"

Favro turned to Pattie. "How fast can you run that?"

"Twenty minutes if you take me to lunch."

"Make it ten, and I'll bring you lunch from Mario's," he countered.

"You're so romantic."

He winked at her and smiled. She was disappointed as usual. The innocent flirtation between the two of them had been going on for years. This was the longest relationship Pattie had had with a man, if that's what one chose to call it. She felt like a schoolgirl around him, even though she tried desperately to maintain a tough exterior. *"Just one of the boys,"* they would call her. But her feminine side ached when he was near. There were so many times over the years she had felt the chemistry between them.

She often thought about what it would be like to kiss him, to feel his arms around her. But it never seemed to go past a certain point. Favro always put the brakes on with some silly joke or sarcasm. Did he feel anything for her? Was he just flirting? She would give anything to know.

Favro popped another mint into his mouth and poured himself a coffee to mask the smell of whiskey on his breath. He kept his usual distance from Pattie so she wouldn't detect the odor. He wondered often if she did. He didn't care what anyone else thought. But for some reason, Pattie mattered. There was something about her that softened him. He tried not to be the tough street guy when he was around her. He actually did have some manners and tried to display them now and again, in his own awkward way. But only for her.

Favro slouched in the chair across from the chief's desk. He wondered what Beckwith would do with him given all the new information he had dropped in his lap the day before. He took the wooden stir stick out of his coffee and picked at his teeth. Then the stare-down began. Who would flinch first?

Huh! I win! Favro thought as Beckwith finally looked down at his shoes and shoved his hands into his pockets.

"I want you to bring Dan Jacobs in on our serial killer case, and I want you to bring him up to date by the end of the day."

Favro scrunched his brow and gently set his coffee down on the desk. "I don't work with a partner."

"You do now."

"It's my case," Favro snapped back at him.

The chief flew across his desk, toppling his own coffee.

"It's your case?! … Speak up because I want to make sure I heard you right. Exactly what case would that be?! *You* don't have a case! There have been three murders in the past five months, and you've got *jack shit,"* he said, throwing the files down on his desk. "Three murders! And to top that off, he stopped sending the letters to us. You've hit a wall, and we've gotta get our asses in gear. The press is going crazy with this."

"Why do people read newspapers anymore? I mean it's 2031, for cryin' out loud."

"Well, God forbid I entertain a social-media chat with you since you won't even turn on your damn cell!" Chief Beckwith felt his face getting hot. It was not unusual for his blood pressure to rise when Favro was in the room.

"I've got a whole team working on this case. I can't *believe* you call it *yours!* God, why can't you be part of a team for once in your life?!"

"Well, what have they turned up? This *team* of yours? Endless wire-taps that went nowhere. Stake-outs that were fruitless, unless you want to count the horrendous coffee breath that spread like wildfire, with hemorrhoids to match. The *team* hasn't made any headway in the case whatsoever." Reaching inside his leather jacket, Favro pulled an envelope out and tossed it on the desk. "Here's your letters."

"What the fuck?" Beckwith felt like someone had just slapped him across the face.

"He sent them all to my apartment. One for each murder. The same letters you received, same clues. Except for this last one, which he sent only to me. And … apparently to my mail bunk here."

Beckwith sat down and pressed the back of his head firmly against his chair. Long deep breaths ensued while Favro waited for the reckoning.

"Every … one?"

"Since the beginning. His name is Cyrus."

"You know his fucking *name?!* Why didn't you show this to me? I should can your ass *right now* and bring you up on *charges!*"

"I know," Favro said. "But you won't."

"Why the hell not?" he asked, jumping to his feet.

"You know, Chief, you swear way too much. That's probably why you get all those migraines."

"Shut the hell up!" Beckwith yelled. His face was beet red now. "You know how hard it's been trying to piece that postal-murder together without a letter. We got spoiled … We got complacent using those letters. The postal museum makes a total of three deaths! Oh Lord … I'm gonna lose my pension!"

"I'll get him, sir," Favro nodded confidently.

"Women are dying because you're his personal pen pal! How come you know so much and I don't? *I'm the fucking chief of police!!*" he screamed. Beckwith had reached his boiling point. Spit flew from his mouth as he yelled. The arms on his chair almost broke right off as he slammed it around behind his desk. "Why should I trust *anything* you say after what you've just admitted?"

Favro leaned forward in his chair. "Because I have an iron-clad plan that you're gonna help me with, and it's gonna work. Let's be honest … It was me that made the most headway with the first two letters you received. It's how I've come up with this plan."

"Oh, and *now* you need my help. And making the most headway means crap if you didn't *catch* him, you idiot!"

Favro stood up and leaned over the chief's desk. "I'm so close to him now, I can smell his stinking breath." he sneered.

"Yeah. And I can smell yours, and that's trouble enough."

Oops … whiskey breath. Favro pulled back.

"Listen to me, Chief. Don't tell anyone else about the letters or anything we've talked about. I'll be back in one hour to give you all the details. If you don't agree with everything I have to say, then you can bring Jacobs in and do whatever you want with me."

"You bet your ass I will."

"One hour, that's all I ask."

Favro left the station with one thought: *Game on!* He was relieved, actually. It had always only been a matter of time before the chief would have to come into play. He couldn't do this without him.

He climbed inside his 2012 Champion SE. It had been so magnificent when he'd bought it. Black cherry red. The first brand-new car he'd ever owned. The leather bucket seats that used to shine were now cracked and torn. The chrome dash was dented and the paint job was indicative of his driving skills. He'd had the car for nineteen years and made so many custom changes it would make your head spin. The stories it could tell. That superb V8 engine, no longer available in personally owned vehicles, had been converted to a hybrid, which he hated, and then he'd added solar, which he hated more, and which in eight months would be illegal to drive. Some new hydrogen-canola thing he didn't understand. Most of the cars on the road now drove themselves, and others were hybrids designed to handle the new fuel. Parking at docking stations to fully recharge in less than five minutes, they could go six hundred miles easy on one charge. And most people could charge right in their own garage. Even ten years ago, he would never have believed it. He'd done all the work himself on his vehicle, and it was beat to shit just like him. *Fuck! I'll have to get a new car!*

Favro's thoughts wandered. *What kind of car will I get? Maybe a fully automated one, like the Lyra LE. Now that's a luxury car. Doors that open front to back, so I don't fall out when they open. Tinted windows so I can drink and drive anytime I want to. Of course, since they never go over the speed limit, as advanced as they are, they're not really cut out for an undercover cop, an alcoholic, or both.*

So, he would have to pass. *What a shame*, he thought. *How great would it be to type in your destination and catch a twenty-minute power nap! Oh well, who knows what the future will bring.*

He sat there with both hands on the wheel. It wasn't moving. Why wasn't the car moving? Because it was 7:10 a.m., and he only had half a pint under his belt. Reaching under the seat, he pulled out his Tennessee friend and took a long, soothing swig. He didn't look around to see if anyone was watching. Favro didn't hide the fact that he took a drink now and then— more *now* than then. He started the ignition and headed back to his apartment.

Chief Beckwith paced back and forth behind his desk. The phone buzzed, and it startled him.

"What is it, Pattie?"

"The mayor on line one."

Oh, that's just bloody terrific, he thought. "Put him through."

Chief Beckwith straightened his collar and pulled up his pants. You might think he was actually going to have to face the man.

"Paul, it's Jim Campbell."

"Jim, how are you?"

"How am I? Well, I'll tell you what ... I'm not very fucking good. The election is coming, Paul, and I'd kind of like to win. We've got a serial killer on the loose, man. The women in our communities are scared shitless. The media are reporting every day that we have an incompetent police force, and I'm the one taking it up the ass! How's your day?"

"Jim, we're going to catch this guy. In fact, we're very close to breaking the case. He's getting very sloppy."

"Did you say 'sloppy?' Let's talk about that word: 'sloppy.' 'Sloppy' and 'disgusting.' This, by the way, pretty much describes how you and your department have been handling this case!"

"Look, Jim, I have a great team on this case, and we've been sharing everything with the FBI. They haven't made any progress with it either."

"The FBI? This has become a bureau nightmare. You weren't promoted to police chief so you could hand all your cases over to the FBI. That's not how things work anymore, Paul. This is your baby, and he's a big one. He doesn't get any more time-outs, Paul. Spank his fucking ass! Now. Or I'll find someone who will. Got it? Oh, and the next headline I read better be 'Serial Killer Captured.'"

The phone slammed loudly in Beckwith's ear. He pulled his head back from the receiver and winced, thinking twice about the deal he'd made with Favro.

It was eleven-thirty before Favro returned to the station.

"Did you run those numbers, Pattie?"

"Where is my lunch?"

He set the bag down on her desk.

She smiled and handed him the paper. "Just so you know, I did have it ready in ten minutes."

Dramatically, he slapped his hands together into a praying position. "Pattie, I love you."

"Piss off," she said, throwing her pen at him.

Favro could see Detective Jacobs sitting in the chief's office. *Ahh … Right on schedule.* He casually sauntered over and into the office.

"Well, if it isn't Mr. *I'll be back in one hour.*"

"I had important police business to do, Chief."

"Really? Well, as of right now, you have a partner."

"Good. I need one."

Beckwith put his hands on his hips and scrunched his brow. "I'm gonna kill somebody today."

Favro looked straight at him. "You can start with me. Cyrus has to think I'm dead for this plan to work. So … I'm going to have an accident. A bad one. That's where we're gonna start. He's gonna get really mad when he finds out I'm gone, Chief, and he's gonna screw up big time. Without him keeping tabs on me, I'll be able to track him, move in, and catch him."

Favro wasn't sure yet about the twisted bond Cyrus felt he had with him, but he expected Cyrus would break his pattern when he found out he was dead. He'd been taking pleasure in playing "the game," and serial killers just don't quit.

Jacobs sat on the edge of his chair, looking like he wanted to bolt out of the office. *Why did this have to be my first homicide case?* he thought.

Beckwith wasn't convinced. "Jesus Murphy! That's it? *That's* your plan? How do you know he's not gonna go ape-shit and start doubling his quota?"

"I don't like it, and I don't want to be involved," Jacobs said then, speaking up for the first time. "What if something happens to you and Internal finds out? *I'm* gonna be swimming in the tank."

Favro tipped his chin, looking steely eyed at him. "You just got involved."

The field outside Stonebrook Penitentiary was jam-packed with protesters and self-proclaimed vigilantes. As the chaplain dressed himself for the day, his thoughts wandered. What had previously been the death-row holding cell today played host to Edgar Sanderson and history in the making.

He had made this walk many times in the past thirty-two years, but he was certain that today it would seem a mile long. His sermon to "the soon to die" was always the same, and he had a biblical answer for pretty much any question an inmate might put forth. However, the Narcoleptic Sleep Tank and Chambers were new to him as well. This morning, he prayed hard for the knowledge and the words to answer Edgar's questions. He prayed for his soul as well.

What a mess we've made of this world, he thought. *God is all forgiving, but He would surely be shaking His head upon us today.* He asked the guard if Edgar had made a last-meal request.

"T-bone steak, rare, hot dog with the works, and a big piece of banana-cream pie," he answered. "And two cigarettes."

Oh Lord, please give me the words ...

Twenty-four witnesses would be allowed in to view Edgar Sanderson carry out his sentence. Once he was in the tank, it would all be up to him.

Chief Beckwith rose in the morning with heaviness in his chest. Something was troubling him greatly. It was more than the deal he'd made with Favro. He didn't feel good. As the police chief, it was his duty to be in attendance for the "carrying out" of the first sentence in the Narcoleptic Sleep Tank. One wouldn't think something like this would cause a former homicide detective to squirm. But that morning, he would have traded jobs with the janitor if it meant getting out of going.

Fifteen of the witnesses present were from the media, though no cell phones had been allowed. There were six members of Audrey Madison's family, all of whom were inconsolable. Edgar's mother and aunt were present, and then Beckwith. The only thing on everyone's mind was what Edgar would do when he got in the tank.

It was 8:55 a.m. The sentence was to be carried out at nine. Those five minutes seemed like forever to everyone who'd come to bear witness. Beckwith couldn't take his eyes off the draped window, and when the curtain opened suddenly, it startled him. The water tank was enormous and frightening. Beckwith cringed as he considered what was about to take place. *Will he thrash about? Will he look into our eyes? Jesus, I hope not.* It reminded him of the Roman Colosseum days and how they would throw men to the lions.

At precisely nine a.m., the chute at the top of the tank opened and a naked Sanderson slid headfirst into the massive tank of water like a seal. He crossed his arms in a defiant move and held his breath for what seemed like forever.

Edgar's mother's hands flew to her eyes as she tried not to look, but she couldn't help peeking through her fingers. It was like watching a horror movie at the scariest part.

Suddenly, Edgar moved straight to the side of the tank and pushed the black button. A cloudy liquid emerged from a small pipe. Edgar smiled, showing all his teeth, then reached over and smashed down the red button. His mother screamed. Some media members tried to leave, but they were not permitted.

His body stiffened for a moment, then softened like a mermaid in the water. Finally, his body floated slowly to the top of the tank. People were out of their seats. Some were crying, but not for Edgar Sanderson. Their hysteria came from the shock of what they'd just witnessed. The press wrote feverishly.

Then the curtain closed. It was over. It was official. The first person in the Tank had taken his own life.

Chief Beckwith slowly made the walk back to his car. He had parked far away on purpose. No hurry to get there and no hurry to get back to work. He had taken the rest of the day off. The last two days had been trying for him. He'd asked himself over and over, *Can Favro's plan work? Can we even pull this thing off?* There was only one conclusion: At this point, he had nothing to lose, and if anyone could disappear without being noticed, it was Jack Favro.

Walking into the station at seven-thirty that morning, Favro winked once at Pattie and headed toward Beckwith's office. Something was different. Today, she noticed that he walked with a purpose. His head was down.

"What? No hug and kiss?" she asked. She smiled at him, but he didn't smile back. He was going to miss her. *She's the only one who gets my jokes*, he thought.

As Pattie watched Favro and Beckwith shake hands through the glass windows, she couldn't help but think that something wasn't right. It was the first time in nine years she had seen that happen. No … Something was not right.

CHAPTER 4

ANGELA BERG TRIED to rub her eyes without smearing her mascara. *The smoke in this bar is killing me,* she thought. *You'd think by 2031 smoking would be banned in even the shittiest of bars. But oh no! As long as you pay that extra, extra tax to the government, you can smoke in just about any dive you want!* Her clothes reeked of it. But it didn't truly bother her that much. These were her bar-hopping, man-chasing clothes. Her slutty clothes.

Picking up her purse to leave, she didn't notice that her cell phone was missing. As she walked out of the bar, she also didn't notice the man who'd been stalking her within it. This was surprising as she had been trying very hard to get picked up. Reaching the end of the block to cross the street, Angela felt a strong hand on her right shoulder, spinning her around, bringing her face to face with her stalker.

"Excuse me, miss, but you seem to have dropped your cell."

"Oh my God!" she exclaimed. "You scared the shit out of me!"

Her crass language was not a surprise to him. But Cardoso & Steinberg, the law firm she worked for, would never put up with it, or with the way she was dressed. Obviously, a quick change after work spoke to her morality as well. Her "barely there" outfit was giving out signals galore. Cyrus smiled and gazed into her eyes.

Her guard was down immediately. *Those eyes ... she thought. Oh my God, those eyes!* "Thank you. Where did I lose it?" she asked.

"Right here," he lied. "It just slipped right out of your handbag."

His eyes, a silver blue, were stunning under the streetlight. They looked deep into hers, and all of her defenses were down.

Suddenly, he lunged towards her, grabbed her by the arms, and tossed her to the ground. They rolled over and over each other, landing hard against a brick building. A car whizzed by, missing them by inches.

"Holy shit! Are you okay?" she asked breathlessly.

"I'm fine," he said. Releasing his hold on her, Cyrus stood up and helped Angela to her feet.

"I didn't even *see* that car!" she said, trying to regain her composure. "You know what? You just saved my life!"

"Well, we were both lucky."

"Look, could I buy you a drink?" she asked, wasting no time with this superhero.

"I could use one," he said flatly. "But let's make it a coffee. I don't drink."

Hmm ... A handsome, non-drinking superhero who just saved my life? What more could a girl ask for?

"Coffee sounds great."

She slipped her arm through his and smiled.

Screw Happy Hour! Angela thought. *This is the most excitement I've had in years!* "Where would you like to go?"

"Well, I'm staying at the Matriarch just around the corner. I think they have a cafe in the lobby."

Cyrus Bircham was leading the way now, and she was under his spell.

"Are you in town on business?" she asked as they reached the hotel.

"Business. Yes. I travel a lot. It's nice to see a friendly face."

"What do you do for a living?" she asked boldly.

"Mostly public relations." he grinned.

Angela felt no need to pry any further. That sexy grin and those smiling eyes knocked any doubt right out of her head. Most women might be suspicious, but she wasn't. Her instincts hadn't gotten her into any trouble yet.

The hotel was old but wonderfully kept. Intricate carvings of time-honored women throughout the ages adorned the front of the building. Although weathered, they were captivating and magnificent. Joan of Arc, Cleopatra, Florence Nightingale, and Sojourner Truth were among the many who guarded your stay.

"I can't believe it! I haven't even introduced myself." Unleashing her hold on his arm, she shoved her hand toward him. "I'm Angela Berg."

He fibbed again, giving her his best shy smile. "Tom … Tom Lancaster."

As they reached the lobby, he turned to her. "The cafe seems to be closed. Shall I walk you back to your car?"

"Don't you have a coffee maker in your room?" she asked, tipping her head and smiling.

"Well, yes, actually I do. Will you join me?"

"I can't wait," she cooed.

She was flirting shamelessly with him now but couldn't help it. It was too exciting. "I wouldn't mind freshening up a bit.

My jacket is an awful mess, and I snagged my hosiery when we took that tumble together." She lifted her skirt just high enough to show a little thigh.

"Look …" she whined. "These are completely ruined."

Cyrus never fancied himself a catch-and-release type of fisherman. He liked the filleting process too much. Besides, he'd barely had to cast, and this gal had swallowed the whole hook. She wasn't a nibbler. He had to keep her now. He moved closer, looking deep into her eyes.

"Yes, well, we'll get you straightened up when we get to my room."

Angela almost fainted. No man had ever looked at her the way he'd just done. In the elevator, he kept his hands to himself, his back to the wall and arms outstretched with hands firmly on the grab bar behind him. With his ankles crossed, he was picture perfect for a magazine cover. Cyrus used his sexiest smile again (dimples and all) to toy with her, and it was working. Angela couldn't stand still. She was squirming all over the place. She wanted him to kiss her, but he wouldn't let go of that damn bar, making the elevator ride, which was only moments, seem like an eternity.

As he swung the door open to his suite, her mind was racing. She couldn't help thinking, *this guy either has a major expense account, or a lot of money!* The suite was luxurious. Truthfully, her lonely life had seen a lot of hotel rooms, and although she had never been here before, this had to be one of their finest suites! She was sure of it!

It had a full bar, and not the kind with those little bottles. Crystal decanters left rainbows on the ceiling. The wingback chairs were button-tuck satin in a sky blue, and a steel-blue leather sofa called her name. *The draperies … Oh my God, the draperies!* This was as sexy as it gets. Although feeling like she didn't deserve all this, Angela was practically salivating, and the smell of fresh coffee brewing made her feel privileged as she was far more used to the smell of whiskey and old carpet. This was the best "date" of her life.

"Can I use your toi— I mean, your powder room?"

"Absolutely. It's the first door to your right."

Once in the confines of the lavish bathroom, she fumbled through her purse for a condom. *A smart girl is always prepared,* she thought as she pulled off her torn pantyhose and sprayed on a light mist of cheap perfume. *Wait till the girls at work hear about this! A little lipstick, and ready for love.*

As she opened the door to the bathroom, the blow came hard—right across the bridge of her nose. Angela flew backwards, smashing her head against the opulent sink. Blood spattered into the air.

Cyrus hissed. "You stupid bitch." He grabbed her ankles and dragged her into the hall. His destination … the bedroom.

Reeling from the blow, she saw the tin ceiling tiles in the hallway pass swiftly over her head. Blood trickled into her eyes and mouth. Her vision was blurred, and she could no longer speak. She clawed at the walls of the hallway, leaving trails in the antique wallpaper. Her attempts to free herself were feeble. She could taste her own blood now. His strength was enormous, and she was weakening by the second. By the time they reached the bedroom, disorientation and exhaustion had disabled her completely.

"It's going to be a long night, my dear. Let's get a little cozy, shall we?" Pulling her up onto the bed, Cyrus stared at his conquest. "Where to start?" he pondered aloud. "Where … to … start."

Shaking his head with one hand on his chin, a sickening grin formed between the two little dimples on his face. Then he used his thumb to smear her red lipstick across her cheek before putting a strip of duct tape over her mouth. And then he pounced.

Angela could feel his weight upon her, and then pain ripping through her insides. Her eyes were swollen shut now. There had been no need to tie her up. He was strong, and she had no power to fight. Cyrus was hitting her over and over again, but not with his fists. That's all she remembered before passing out. It would be her last memory.

Favro's apartment was as plain-Jane as it comes. If you didn't know better, you might think it had been hit with a bazooka. What an explosive mess. Someone who didn't give a shit definitely lived there. It had no personality whatsoever. No pictures on the side tables or slippers on the floor. In the living room, a built-in flat screen was the only semblance of company he might have. He had towels for drapes and a mangy couch that looked like it served more as a bed than for entertaining. Empty pizza boxes and booze bottles decorated the hardwood floor.

The small kitchen had the basic essentials, but that was about it: a coffee maker and a microwave. Coffee grounds splayed across the counter, and loads of dishes littered the sink despite the dishwasher. There weren't any magnets on the fridge, or police-car-shaped salt-and-pepper shakers, personalized coffee mugs, or a favorite cereal in the cupboard. In fact, he barely had any food at all. Now, the tea towel on his stove was interesting. It read: "Be kind to animals or I'll kill you." Oookay … Another unsolved mystery in the life of Jack Favro.

In his bedroom, he lay on his unmade bed. A brand-new letter from Cyrus had arrived. Before opening the envelope, he couldn't help but wonder, *Is he killing her right now or is she still alive?* He examined it carefully. Once sifting through all the self-righteousness and bragging, he managed to find three good clues. Inside the envelope was a "Do Not Disturb" sign, a reference to Joan of Arc, and a sentence in quotation marks that read: "You can hear her scream when the bell tolls."

He packed the letter in an eight by ten metal box that already contained several scraps of notepaper, a journal, and photocopies of the other letters from Cyrus. He would have to share this new letter with the Chief so he could give it to the other detectives working the case.

His duffel bag was full now. He had taken an hour to tidy up and gotten rid of all the pizza boxes and liquor bottles, making sure to check all his hiding spots. He'd never understood why he hid his liquor when he lived alone, but he did. He took one last look around. Catching a glimpse of himself in the hall mirror, he knew his looks would soon change. Slicked back hair and grown-out scruffy beard wouldn't be enough. He would probably have to shave his head.

Giving up his leather jacket would be the hardest; he was definitely having a little separation anxiety where that was concerned. A jean jacket with a leather collar would have to do for now. His new residence would be a motel room that was big enough to work in and call home, but shitty enough not to draw attention.

Favro drove his car the twenty minutes to Oak Bluff Ravine, did what he had to do, and then parked off a side road to wait for Jacobs. His hands were shaking. He needed a drink. He reached for the flask inside his jacket but didn't get a chance to indulge. Tires crunched on the gravel road as Jacobs pulled in right on schedule.

"Are you ever late?!" he shouted, stepping into the headlights of Jacobs's car, an immaculately kept 2029 Lennox convertible—a wedding gift from his father-in-law.

"Well now, let's see ... There may come a time when tardiness is in order, perhaps an elegant dinner party or fancy soiree of some sort, but not when I've got a fucking cadaver in the trunk of my car!"

"Brought your wife, did you?" Favro laughed.

"Hey! That's not even funny! Can we please just get on with this! And *you're* taking it out of the trunk, by the way. I almost died myself just getting it in there."

"Jesus, Jacobs, how did you ever make Homicide?"

"Excuse me, but digging up dead people and tossing them in the trunk of my car wasn't part of my training. I thought that's what we were supposed to catch the *bad* guys doing."

He opened the trunk, and they both stood over the body.

"Hmm, a little stinky, isn't he?" Favro asked.

"Oh ... I'm sorry. Was I supposed to pick the one that smelled good? They just laid the grass on him this morning. And you owe me a new suit jacket," Jacobs snapped.

"What the hell for?"

"I left mine in the coffin."

Favro raised his brow. "Why? Was he chilly?"

"I threw up on it, okay? Thought I'd give it the burial it deserved. Let's hurry up." Jacobs's patience was gone. He was afraid of getting caught now.

"You puked? Jesus, *that's* what stinks so bad!" Favro laughed.

"Can we please get this over with, for crying out loud?"

"Alright, alright ... Calm down."

"Have you got the skid marks right?"

"I'm not an amateur like you," Favro bragged.

Truth be told, he'd almost gone over the cliff while skidding the car earlier. But he would never admit that to Jacobs.

With the body in place, and the car dowsed with gas, Favro tossed his badge on the front seat and lit the match. One easy push and over she went in a blazing inferno. He wasn't a crier, but watching his Champion go up in flames almost did it for him. It was at least two hundred feet to the bottom of the ravine, and the explosion when it hit lit up the night sky ... *No turning back now. Game on.*

Jacobs drove Favro to his new digs, the Rocky Bottom Motel and Bar, where they waited for his cell to ring. Nearly six hours went by before that call came in at 2:18 a.m., startling them both as they dozed. Jacobs flew out of his chair, and Favro thought he was going to pull his gun. He laughed out loud. After a quick conversation, Jacobs turned to his partner.

"Seems one of Washington's finest homicide detectives has died in a car accident. The license plate identified his car, and his badge was recovered. It was Detective Jack Favro. Of course, the body was burned beyond recognition. Chief Beckwith wants me to handle the investigation personally, seeing as we were partners and all."

"Well, don't waste any time," Favro grinned. "We wouldn't want a lot of detectives nosing around the crash site, and I certainly don't want anyone checking dental records." There was silence between the two of them for a moment.

"He was an outstanding detective, wasn't he?"

"Actually, I thought he was a bit of an asshole," Jacobs replied. "I plan on doing the eulogy myself."

They both laughed. *Finally!* Favro thought. *This boy is loosening up a little.*

"You have my new number, right?"

"I got it," Jacobs replied.

Cyrus is going to be so pissed off when he reads this in the paper, Favro thought. He hoped. Speaking of pissed, he couldn't wait any longer for a drink and practically pushed Jacobs out the door. He proceeded to get wrecked on single malt while sorting out his notes. He stared at his new driver's license. "Phillip Caruso," he said out loud. *Sounds like an opera singer.*

Favro re-read the most recent letter from Cyrus, again and again. "Do Not Disturb" was obvious: a hotel or motel. The last two clues were not as easy though. "Joan of Arc" and "You can hear her scream when the bell tolls." What did they mean? Other than the obvious, of course. Someone was going to die … assuming they weren't already dead. This much he could count on.

He was groggy and stumbling at this point and made his way toward the bed. He didn't want to wake up on the floor again. He slowly dozed off.

The news of Favro's "death" spread rapidly throughout the department. His accident was received with mixed reviews. Chief Beckwith met with Detective Jacobs to talk about the next course of action. There are many things to tend to when an officer dies while on duty. Jacobs needed to leak it to the media so it would be in the morning paper.

Some officers weren't the least bit surprised. He'd obviously hit the sauce too much, misjudged the corner at the embankment, and just sailed right over. They knew that he was adopted and an only child, and that his adoptive parents were gone … so there wasn't even anyone to notify. Open and shut investigation. Most just bitched about the added caseloads they would have to take on.

Despite the number of years he'd worked for the department, Favro had made few friends. He was a loner both on and off the job. When he wasn't working, he contemplated cases and drank. When he worked, he had a steely mind for cracking cases wide open. And he drank. He had never worked with a partner, unless you counted his Tennessee friend. Whiskey was his only companion.

It wasn't that everyone disliked him. They just didn't put themselves out there like he did, taking stupid risks. Favro wasn't afraid to get his hands dirty or put his neck on the line. He did things the old-fashioned way. His sort of detective was almost extinct, leaving him the last of his species. It had bothered some of the guys that his leather jacket had some blood spatter on one arm that wasn't his. Would it have made a difference if it had been? Probably not. A badge of honor perhaps? He didn't wear it proudly though. He just wore it, and it bothered them.

The Cyrus case fell solely on the rest of the "team" now. But every lead led them nowhere. They just had no fire in their bellies. Maybe they *should* be called sloppy, like the mayor had said. The chief wasn't exactly pushing them, which was even worse because he now had all his eggs in Favro's basket. Favro's and that "wienie" Jacobs.

And then there was Pattie. *Oh God ... Pattie.* Chief Beckwith knew this would be a terrible blow to her and wanted to be the one to tell her, as much as he dreaded the task. He wondered if she had already heard the news. She had worked under him in the same precinct for twelve years, and when you spend that much time around someone, you know a little bit about them. He knew she cared about Favro. He knew she would take it hard. Beckwith hadn't factored in this part of the plan—the part where he would have to hurt someone. He watched the clock. At five minutes to six, he walked to her desk and waited. *Lord, let her call in sick ... just once.*

Pattie, of course, was right on time as usual. Her demeanor told him that she didn't know. He asked her to come to his office. A few moments later, everyone watched through the glass windows as she collapsed into his arms. She was inconsolable, and he had one of the officers drive her home. There was no turning back now. Favro was dead, but he was also in charge. Beckwith felt nauseous.

Favro's cell phone went off at nine a.m., and his head was pounding as usual. He scrambled for his cell, bumping his forehead on the nightstand in the process.

"Mother Fu—What? What the hell is it?"

"Good morning, Mr. Caruso," Jacobs chirped. "I trust you slept well."

He groaned. "Didn't you just leave here?"

"Listen up. They picked up a call from the Matriarch Hotel. It looks like we're in business."

Matriarch Hotel. Joan of Arc.

"While we were bumping you off last night, Cyrus was making good on the last letter he sent you."

Favro was wide awake now.

"She was beaten up big time and raped also."

"Raped? That's not Cyrus's M.O."

"It is now. It had his signature."

"How so?"

"There was a 'Do Not Disturb' sign on the body."

Favro was standing now, and the cobwebs were clearing quickly.

"Are you sitting down?" Jacobs asked then.

"No."

"Well, you might want to for this one. The medical examiner was poking away at her this morning when she heard a noise coming from the body."

"What the hell kind of noise?" Favro's eyes widened.

"Well, more specifically, a ringing sound. That sick fuck pushed a cell phone up inside her vagina and called first thing this morning."

There was silence on Favro's end for a moment. *When the bell tolls.* Then he snapped, "Tell me no one answered it!"

"Oh yeah ... She just reached up inside, pulled it out, and said, 'Good Morning, chief medical examiner's office?' ... I don't think so," Jacobs said sarcastically.

"Well, find out for sure, and if he calls back, make sure they don't answer it," Favro said.

"What the hell is going on in your head?" Jacobs asked.

"The same thing that should be going on in yours. 'Hear her scream when the bell tolls!' That phone belongs to someone. I think he has another victim that he's keeping alive, and if you answer that cell from Angela Berg's body, I think you're going to hear him kill her."

"It was a burner phone, Fav, the one in Angela. There's no way to trace it."

"Well, get it! I don't want anyone near it but us. Get it today!"

CHAPTER 5

TO SAY THAT Cyrus's 1940s bungalow on Travers Lane was charming would not do it justice. It was exquisite. It had two bedrooms, one bath, a dining room, living room, large kitchen, and a full basement. It was kept tidy and decorated almost like a fishing lodge rather than a city house. Dark cherry paneling covered the walls in the living room. The dining-room walls had cream wainscoting and were adorned with blue and white china plates, all in different sizes and shapes. A long oak table that could seat twelve, with matching chairs, were the room's only contents.

The kitchen, however, was its jewel. Dark blue ceramic pans and copper pots hung from a rack on the ceiling. The entire floor was made of one-inch, black and white ceramic tiles, shiny and smooth. The intertwining deer-antler light fixture over the table was odd, yet perfect in the setting. The cupboards were cream-colored with black trim to match the wainscoting and had clear-glass doors to display the old china. It looked like a picture out of a magazine: perfectly staged. An old ceramic cookstove of the same color and era matched spot on, with an antique copper kettle sitting on top, shining like the day it was forged. A small oak table with rounded spindle chairs and a cream-colored island with a butcher block top finished the look. The window over the porcelain sink was partially open, and a cool breeze blew the gingham drapes inward.

Down the hall, things were a little different. The first bedroom was a perfect match in decor with the rest of the house. The second bedroom, however, contained only a single wrought-iron bed and a light bulb hanging from an unfinished fixture. Cyrus lay there peacefully. Newspaper clippings and paper copies of Posts and Facebook chats papered the ceiling above him.

All the newspaper clippings from *The D.C. Liberty* were arranged in the order they'd originally been reported. From the very first woman he'd murdered under a year ago, right down to the dissatisfaction expressed towards the Washington, D.C., police department and their unsuccessful efforts to capture the killer.

Cyrus was old school. He loved the newspaper, and although he wondered if they would ever become ancient history, he knew it would never happen in his lifetime. A world without *The Washington Post* or *The Wall Street Journal*, for example, was hard to imagine. People still wanted to smell that fresh ink. They wanted to cut out their loved ones' obituaries and tuck them away, then find them years later, stuck in an old book or drawer somewhere and say "AWWW."

He'd actually had a paper route in his late teens. It had been the only steady thing in his life. He'd wrapped all his dead animals in them and left them on the doorsteps of people who didn't pay him on time. Even then, he could command fierce attention when needed. And he'd needed a lot.

Cyrus stared at the light bulb over his head and smiled to himself. Soon the morning paper would arrive, and he was certain to add another article to his shrine of self-worship. He wondered how much sleep Favro was losing over the clues he'd left with Angela Berg's body. Laughing aloud, he clapped his hands together and could barely compose himself.

He rose from the bed and promptly straightened his clothes, and then the covers, in that order. Pulling the blanket and sheet taut, his long fingers gently smoothing out all the wrinkles, his hand moved on to the pillow, puffing it up to its original shape. Satisfied, he smiled. But that would soon change.

The morning paper was officially twenty minutes late. He struggled not to check his cell. He wanted the hard copy of *The D.C. Liberty*. He was imagining what the headline would be. He was imagining slitting the paper boy's throat for making him wait. He paid that kid a lot of money to deliver at exactly the same time every morning. Home delivery barely even existed anymore. He was just grateful that the newspaper he wanted still had it. His patience was wearing thin though, and he could wait no longer.

Cyrus made his way to the bathroom. He splashed water on his face and combed his perfect hair into its perfect style. Happy with his plain but modern clothes, he headed to the small truck-stop down the road.

As he walked in the door, all heads turned his way. This did not alarm him in the least. Cyrus didn't have that "I'm a truck driver and damn proud of it!" look. Though he appeared much more refined, he used his mastery to fit into a crowd. It worked. Within seconds, the small group went back to chatting and drinking their coffee.

He slid onto the stool at the counter. The waitress came to take his order, her puffy body squished into a uniform two sizes too small. Her slaughter of the English language made him want to stick his butter knife into her belly, turn it, and run it straight up to her throat. He decided against it but was soon reconsidering as she made a painful attempt at humor. "Hey, Ken! Where's Barbie?" she said a little too loudly.

"Hmm … Yes, very good," he stated. "Would you kindly bring me a cup of Earl Gray tea with an extra pot of hot water? Also, I would like a copy of today's newspaper please."

"Well, you can get your paper yourself, little man. Right at the front door if you want it."

She took a step back and stared at him calmly. "I know what you done," she said slyly.

Cyrus's expression didn't change, but his breathing stopped.

"I can feel it. They're still cryin' too. I can tell. You done broke a lot of women's hearts, mister!" she sneered, and then started laughing—or (more accurately) snorting.

Cyrus exhaled slowly.

"Why, my Henry would kill me if he caught me even lookin' at you. I know all about you and what you done, so you can just keep those grabby hands to yourself!" she said, winking and snorting away.

He glanced at her name badge, and then held her gaze. He didn't even blink. Finally, her brow crinkled, and the coffee cup started to shake in her hand.

"Hell, mister, can't you take a joke?"

Cyrus reached for "Edna's" hand across the counter. Slowly, he raised the bloated appendage to his lips and kissed it softly. He told her that Henry was a very lucky man, and then asked for his tea to go. He picked up the newspaper on his way out the door, leaving Edna with her mouth wide open and nothing going in or out for the first time in her life.

Pattie hit the alarm button before it went off. Her internal clock woke her every morning at just about the same time. So many years at the station had made her a lady of routine. She wasn't sure if this was good or bad. However, putting one foot in front of the other and blazing forward seemed just the right thing to do.

Her four-poster, white-iron bed was an antique. The all-white linen and tiny pink flowers on the quilt gave softness to the room. It was exactly what you would expect to see in Pattie's bedroom. Very ladylike. She slipped her legs out from under the sheet and swung her feet over the edge of the bed.

Sitting there, wiggling her toes, she found herself crying … again. Maxwell lay purring beside her as usual. The regal Russian Blue was her closest companion. He barely left her side. If she was getting up for breakfast, so was he.

Some might say that Pattie's condo was small, but for her, it was just right. She had been a renter most of her life, but when she'd spotted this sweet little cottage-style condo for sale, she'd changed her mind quickly, thinking, *This could be home sweet home for me and Maxwell.* Granny had left her a nice inheritance—enough to pay for the condo as well as some comfy pieces of furniture and odds and ends to start making it feel like home.

The deck off the living room was spacious, and the potted plants and flowers added so much color. Pansies, marigolds, petunias, and impatiens were her signature. And let's not forget the yellow roses. Those were her favorite. There was even a time one had showed up on her desk at work. Only a detective would know about her preference, but not a word was ever said.

In her garden, Pattie even grew a little catnip for Maxwell. She thought of everything. She always thought of everything and everyone before herself.

Through feelings of despair, she forged ahead. She pulled a housecoat on over her silky pajamas. Her dark hair rested in a long, tidy braid down her back. Once she got to the kitchen,

Pattie poured herself a bowl of cereal. She had the same thing every day: her favorite, Rice Krispies and a banana. Then she grabbed a bowl to give Maxwell his breakfast.

Coffee was the next order of the day, preparing it before work like she always did, but this wasn't just any other workday, and it wouldn't ever be again without Jack. Her bottom lip began to quiver.

"Oh, Jack, I miss you so much," she said aloud. It had only been a few days since Favro's passing. *"Fight the good fight"* might be the motto at work, but all she could do was fight back tears.

Pattie paused as Maxwell twirled between and around her ankles, purring and rubbing his whiskers against her. There, in the kitchen, she thought for a moment. *Will I be able to get through this day? With the love of my life gone forever?* She headed for the shower. She was on a self-proclaimed mission. Don't show, don't tell, and don't feel … Be tough. There was no other way to get through each day now.

Patricia O'Rourke had lived in Washington, D.C., all her life, taking criminal-justice courses in university. Two years in, she'd dropped out with no drive to be a lawyer as planned. Then she'd done a two-year stint on Pennsylvania Avenue with the D.C. Department of Juvenile Justice. But even as a paper pusher, there were just too many nightmares over those kids, and she hadn't been content.

Finally, she'd found herself working at the precinct where Chief Paul Beckwith had ended up, and she was pleased. Pattie was appreciated there, and that made her loyal. She was making a good life for herself, but it was not quite as exciting as she'd hoped … until she'd met Jack Favro. She had dated men on and off over the years, but for the last nine, she'd been in love with only one. The only problem with that relationship was that he wasn't in it with her.

After her shower, she dried her long hair and re-braided it to put it up in a bun. Tears welled up in her big brown eyes. All those years she'd loved him and never told him. Why? All the joking, the chemistry between them ... She knew he'd felt it too. He had to. It couldn't have just been her. He'd never said anything to her though, so what good was it? Right?

She knew she had to move forward with her life now, get on with things, and get over him. Be tough. The chief and the new detective, Dan Jacobs, kept her busy during the workdays. It was the evenings when she was alone that were hard, but soon enough, the evenings would become more adventurous and exciting than she could have ever possibly imagined.

The next day, Pattie contemplated the night ahead. This year, the Policeman's Ball was a costume party, and against her better judgment, she was going to attend. The past few days had been devastating, just trying to come to grips with Favro's death. The accident had her crying every day, but she knew that it was time to mingle with someone other than Maxwell.

Pattie had always wanted to go to a costume party and had made up her mind to have fun. She picked out a Spanish flamenco costume and used a crimping iron on her hair, which fell softly to her waist. She always wore it in a bun at work and doubted anyone at the party would even recognize her once she put her eye mask on.

Her green satin dress with black lace was stunning. The formfitting bustier was snug with the laces done up tight and her décolletage rather revealing. It felt nice to escape for the evening. Maybe she'd even meet someone interesting and try out her social skills. She was definitely a little rusty in that department. She would do her very best not to think about Favro.

The hall was packed with different characters and personalities as she made her way to the punch bowl to mingle. Some of the costumes were elaborate, and some were just plain silly. However, there was one in particular that caught her eye. Zorro was standing by himself, his hat tipped downward to help his mask cover his face. *I wonder if I know him.*

"I couldn't flirt with a rock," she mumbled. "But here goes nothing."

Pattie grabbed a glass of champagne off the table and decided it was time to become better acquainted. This was definitely not her style, but if losing Jack had taught her anything, it was that it's now or never. As she made a beeline toward Zorro, a Blue Boy stepped in her path.

"Care to dance, senorita?"

That voice, I know it, she thought. "Chief, is that you?"

"Yeah, it's me. It was either this or Napoleon, and I didn't feel like keeping my hand shoved in my coat all night."

He looked at her differently. "Pattie, you look so pretty … I had no idea your hair was that long."

"I don't think anybody does … but thank you for the compliment."

"Well," he said teasingly, "all I can say is that it's a good thing I'm married. If you're not with anyone, you're welcome to join Cathy and me. Front-row table. The ceremony is starting soon."

Geez, am I that pathetic he just assumes I don't have a date?

Pattie glanced over his shoulder. Zorro had vanished.

"I would love to join you," she said. "It's been a long time since I've seen Cathy."

The tables were captivating, with white linens, low-light candles, and tall vases of red-dragon calla lilies. She would have loved to have a strong arm to hold onto tonight. The lights brightened, and the music stopped. Briar Rabbits and Cinderellas were scrambling to their seats. George Washington stepped up to the podium, and even with his flour-colored wig, there was no mistaking the mayor's voice.

"Welcome, ladies and gentlemen, to the sixty-first Washington, D.C., Metropolitan Police Department's annual ball. As you all know, 2031 has been quite a year for the department. The Narcoleptic Sleep Tank and its Chambers have made a significant change to our penitentiary system. Make no mistake though, it has been the fine work of the MPD and all the workforce sitting here tonight that has made for such a successful year. May we have a round of applause, please?" Everyone obliged.

"I would like to take a minute now and ask for everyone to join me in a moment of silence for those who have passed or lost their lives this year in the line of duty. Ladies and gentlemen, please rise."

Pattie's thoughts wandered to Favro, and she felt her eyes welling up with tears again. *Get ahold of yourself!* she thought. With a quick excuse, she made haste from the table and a beeline to the ladies' room. She could hold back no longer. Once inside the safety of the stall, she broke down weeping. *Clearly, it's time to go,* she thought. *This was a bad idea.*

Slipping out of the ball was easy. Though it was early in the evening, most of Washington's finest were three sheets to the wind. It was dark outside. Standing on the sidewalk, Pattie struggled for the code to her car. She felt a hand on her shoulder and turned. Zorro was looking down at her.

"Leaving so soon?" he whispered.

"I ... I'm not in the party mood tonight, I guess."

She could feel her cheeks burning. He stepped closer and lifted his mask.

"How about a late dinner at Mario's?"

Pattie felt her knees go weak as she stared straight into the eyes of a dead man. After a moment, she managed to choke out, "Favro?"

He curled his arm around her waist to keep her from falling. Raising a finger to her lips, Favro didn't say a word. She put her hands on his chest and felt his strength as he pulled her close. Bringing her chin up to meet his, their lips locked in a passionate kiss, their tongues dancing slowly together. Her wish had finally come true. Pattie's ears were ringing, but when she opened her eyes, she burst into tears, seeing her alarm clock ringing loudly next to her bed.

The dream had felt so real, but her green satin dress was nothing more than a nightgown, and there was no costume party ... nor any party at all.

Favro lay staring at the old ceiling fan above his bed. It seemed to spin in slow motion. The alcohol was sweet upon his tongue now, a feeling uncommon to the novice drinker. His thoughts were wandering in every direction, but for some reason, they kept drifting back to Pattie.

He missed their daily banter and found himself missing her lovely smile too. Not a lot of people smiled at him on a regular basis. She was consistent. His eyes found the old fan again, the blades covered in dust. His mother had been meticulous about dusting ... and polishing. He found himself remembering how much time she would spend polishing the small bit of silver she possessed, and the porcelain figurines her mother had left her ... He was drunk now.

He remembered his mother's stunning features, and how (for his twelfth birthday) she'd baked the biggest cake he had ever seen. You could tell it was homemade because it slanted slightly to one side, but even though it was crooked, it had been a sight. And she had made green icing just like he'd ordered.

When he was little, she would tell him stories over hot chocolate at bedtime. She would talk about Paris and how she could have been a big-time opera singer if she'd wanted to, but had given it all up to be a mommy, as she'd loved him so very much.

Favro remembered her long neck, and the single strand of pearls that she never took off. She'd always worn high heels, even in the house and even after working a long shift at the dress shop. She was always smiling, and rubbed his back when he couldn't sleep.

Favro's father had worked nights as a janitor and came home smelling like antiseptic. He would sleep the whole day, and his mother would say that it was because he worked so hard, but even as a child, he'd known that it was because he was drunk. Just after he turned sixteen, his father had taken a swipe at his mother during an argument that had started over the red lipstick she'd come home wearing from work one day.

"The color of whores!" his father had screamed. Meanwhile, he had come home with worse on his shirt collar more than once.

Favro had become a man that day. Finding his hidden strength, he'd struck his father square between the eyes with the first closed fist he'd ever made. His father would never lay a hand on her again. That was the night—the night he'd decided that he wanted to be a cop … to stop everything horrible he'd seen growing up, every cycle of violence, everywhere he saw it, anyway he could. A tall order for a sixteen-year-old, but he'd certainly earned the ambition.

Two years after that, his mother had died of breast cancer, breaking his heart—Favro's, that is. He and his father never spoke much after the funeral, and the old man had died shortly after Jack turned eighteen. They'd found him unconscious in his truck, parked a half-mile from home. The EMTs had never been able to revive him, which had come as a tremendous relief to Favro. Jack had hated his guts and never even held a funeral for him. He had just put his ashes in a coffee can, poked holes in the lid, and late one night, punted it over the Redburn Bridge … not even looking back to see if it sank.

That same night, Favro had gone to a twenty-four-hour drive-through liquor mart and bought a pint of whiskey, driven home, and then poured himself a full glass. Down it went, and up it came. The compulsion of the mind and body took flight.

He fell in love that night, and it had haunted him ever since. A love affair that would ease his pain but also cause more than he could possibly imagine. A reminder of his father, every single day.

Now, with his own funeral coming up in four days, it gave him an eerie feeling. Having been adopted, and not having had any siblings, he couldn't help but wonder who would attend. *Now I'll find out who my real friends are*, he thought in a drunken stupor.

But there was only one person he was really looking forward to seeing: Cyrus. He *knew* Cyrus would be there. After all, they had become such close friends. Cyrus wasn't stupid. He would want to see a funeral procession, people mourning with real tears, and the ashes put in the ground.

Even after all that, Favro knew it didn't guarantee anything. He only prayed that Cyrus wouldn't react by going on a murdering rampage. He wanted him to come out of the shadows and break his pattern, but he didn't want him to do it that way. That would be bad. Very bad.

The last thing he remembered before passing out was wrapping up a little package and putting Pattie's name and address on it.

As Cyrus walked home, he tried to juggle his tea in one hand and read the morning headline with the other. Impossible. The tea was hot, and the paper was not cooperating. He decided to save the newspaper until he could really enjoy it and shoved it under his arm.

His bungalow was four blocks away—an inconspicuous home with a large yard and many trees to shade it. He also owned the houses on either side of it. Nobody lived in them. He took pleasure in his privacy and went to great measures to keep it. Those empty homes and their yards were neatly tended. They must not look abandoned, as this would draw attention, something Cyrus didn't care for. In his spare time, he was a very good repairman and groundskeeper.

He was walking double time back to his house now, and if it weren't for the tight lid on the tea, he would surely have scalded himself. His excitement to read the paper could hardly be contained. Cyrus could slit your throat without breaking a sweat, but reading about it and knowing Favro would be doing the same was beyond exhilarating.

He unlocked the door and shoved his way through the screen. Finally! Spreading *The D.C. Liberty* across the kitchen table, his eyes were glued to the front page. Nothing! Nothing about Angela Berg. Page 2 … Nothing … Page 3 … Washington, D.C., Detective Dies: Detective Jack Favro Killed in Skid Accident off Oak Bluff Ravine.

He slowly clenched his hands around the paper, white knuckled and shaking. As he read the rest of the article, he loosened his grip slowly. Inhaling and holding his breath for a moment as he gritted his teeth, he finally emptied his lungs loudly.

"Oh no, no, no …! You're not going to get off this easily, Mr. Man!" Cyrus went back to the paper to check the obituary section. He wrote down the time and place to attend the funeral. He was going to pay his last respects … in blood.

CHAPTER 6

EVER WONDER WHAT would happen if you just didn't show up for work one day? Would anybody notice? That's exactly what happened to Louise Richards. And nobody did. The publishing company she worked for was huge. Her desk sat empty for two whole days before anyone even questioned her whereabouts. It's not that people didn't notice that she wasn't there. They just didn't care. Louise was a loner. She ate lunch alone and never socialized at office get-togethers. She was a very nice person, as nice goes—a nice person who was scared of her own shadow.

The truth was that Louise suffered from severe social anxiety, and striking up a conversation with someone, anyone, was one of the most painful and terrifying notions she could imagine. So, she'd just plain avoided it at all costs. Her cubicle at work had felt smaller every day. And her colleagues had remained strangers. She'd believed everyone hated her.

So, on that sunny afternoon when she'd asked herself once again, *I wonder if they would even notice if I didn't go back to work*? she'd simply decided to take the afternoon off. Louise hadn't known it then, but it was the rest of her life that she would really be taking off.

When she made eye contact with Cyrus that afternoon, it was the first time in her life she wasn't the first to look away. There was something about his eyes. Why did he hold her gaze? And he smiled at her. My God, he smiled! She couldn't believe it, a man … a stranger, in fact. He wasn't a client. He had no reason to smile at her, but he did.

Immediately, Louise was drawn to him. She couldn't believe it, but now her feet were walking toward him. She even sat down next to him at the little lunch counter at Murphy's. *What am I doing? My God, what am I doing?* She pulled at the neck of her blouse, but of course, a buttoned-up collar wouldn't give much. As nervous as her fingers were, her mouth found courage to spare.

"We're having the same thing!" she blurted out.

"Excuse me?" Cyrus said.

"The Cobb salad! It's delicious, isn't it?" she asked, squirming about in her seat.

And then the wily snake charmer opened his mouth. "Actually," Cyrus smiled, "this is my first time here. I noticed you, and I thought to myself, I just had to have it … The salad, I mean."

Louise burst into a nervous giggle. As innocent as a baby garter snake, she was charmed.

"What's your name?" Cyrus asked in his sexiest voice.

"Louise. What's yours?" She could barely contain herself.

"Albert," he said, completely disingenuous. Lying was second nature to him.

"Really? That's my father's name!" *Oh my God! Did I just say that! Stupid! Stupid! Stupid!*

"Well, I'm flattered to have the same name as your father."

"Oh, I didn't mean anything by that. I mean ... I wasn't saying you were like my father or anything!" Talk about putting your foot in your mouth. Both her socks were soaked!

Cyrus raised a finger to her lips, stopping the chatter immediately. As he pulled his hand away, she reached for him quickly. It was already too late. Louise was smitten, and his fingernail smeared her lipstick.

"I'm so sorry if I've offended you," she said.

"Oh no, not at all," Cyrus said calmly. He couldn't take his eyes off the smeared lipstick. Picking up his napkin, he stared at her face and wiped his own lips. The psychological impact was huge and swift. As if on cue, Louise immediately picked up her own napkin and thoroughly wiped her face, completely cleaning off the smear.

Already proud of the conquest ahead, Cyrus smiled slowly—a sinister smile that should have told her she was dead but didn't. "Would you care to join me for a walk after lunch?" he asked. "Or are you in a hurry to get back to work?"

"Not today," she said. "Today, I'm all yours."

Favro entered the City Lights Lounge. He pulled his hoodie loosely up over his head and slid onto the stool at the end of the bar. The place was smoky and reeked of booze. A real dump. He loved it. He wondered if this was where Cyrus had picked up Angela Berg as the details of the case ran through his mind. In a place like this, the sex trade flowed as freely as the liquor.

As he eyeballed the clientele, the fifteen-foot rule came to mind—the rule that all cops on the street know religiously. If he's got a knife, and you've got a gun, and there are fifteen feet or less between you, remember one thing: a man in motion can get that knife in your jugular faster than you can get a shot off. He knew for sure that every thug in that bar had a knife or a gun. This could pose a challenge for him. He needed to stay alert, but he also needed a drink badly despite having a few under his belt already.

He pulled out the matchbook that had been found in the Matriarch Hotel room. Angela or Cyrus had definitely been in this bar. *How did they meet? What was so charming about him that this woman could be lured so quickly to his hotel room?* And he knew it had been pretty fast because Angela's employer had indicated that she only left work at four p.m.

Now Favro had another woman to find. He knew Cyrus had another woman. He just knew it. A woman Cyrus was longing to kill … longing and waiting. This wasn't Cyrus's usual M.O., and Favro couldn't help wondering why he had broken his pattern and what he was doing with her now. Was he torturing her? Did he have her locked up where her screams couldn't be heard?

"What can I get you?" the bartender asked.

"Whiskey, neat."

He studied the bartender as profiles ran through his head. *Nope, Cyrus doesn't hold a steady job, especially not a night job. He would need too much time off. He wouldn't want people knowing him too well, so he's definitely not a bartender. He can be charming one minute and unapproachable the next, capable of incredible patience when he needed it, yet prone to monstrous outbursts of rage and intolerance at the drop of a hat. He is white, late thirties, early forties. His income is old money, possibly from a trust fund or an inheritance of some kind. But it is substantial. He would need money to do what he does.*

His mother would have left him when he was young. Either by neglect or death. And their time together, though short, would not have been pleasant. Cyrus would have been raised by someone else, maybe an aunt, grandmother, or even a nanny. He would have been neglected badly by them. His need to inflict pain on women and gain superiority over them demonstrates some terrible trauma and abuse as a child, and perhaps even as a young man. He would have been beaten or tortured for sure.

He doesn't do drugs. Cyrus would consider himself too intelligent, and probably didn't even experiment with them growing up. Definitely an only child. He would have to be handsome enough for women to find him attractive but plain enough to blend into a crowd. But what tipped the apple cart? What was it that made him homicidal? The abuse? The torture? What about that extra chromosome theory? Or was it something else?

Why am I so special to him? What part do I play in all this?

Favro tried hard to make his usual mental notes, but the alcohol was impeding his thought process.

"Would you like another one?" the bartender asked.

"Just bring me the bottle."

"Oh, I'm afraid we don't do that here, sir."

"Why not?" Favro asked, shocked that the shitty bar would have such high standards.

"Well, you see, whenever a party of one orders the whole bottle, the evening always ends with me having to introduce them to my old Kentucky friend."

The bartender pulled a baseball bat from behind the counter and showed it to him. Favro read the words "Kentucky Slugger" printed on its side.

"No prejudice where he's concerned," the bartender continued. "Just doing his job. I really hate it when that happens, but he's usually always right."

"Fine, I get the message. Just make it a double."

Favro reached for his cell, which was vibrating in his jacket pocket. He couldn't stand the ring tone. Most times, it was Jacobs anyway.

"Hit me."

"Hit you?" Jacobs asked.

"What is it, you idiot? What do you have?" He never missed an opportunity to pick on his partner.

"Oh, s-sorry," Jacobs stuttered. "I spoke to the medical examiner regarding Angela Berg. The actual cause of death was, uh … Hold on … 'Multiple, severe, intracranial hematomas.' The first strike came to the bridge of her nose, which would have probably knocked her out for a bit. There is some evidence that she hit her head on the bathroom sink, so it may have started in there. She was alive when he raped her and shoved the cell phone in, and probably conscious for some of it."

"That's bloody brutal," Favro said, shaking his head. "What did he hit her with?"

"Well, his fists at first, and a coffee maker the rest of the time. There was a lot of blood and hair all over it, and they found twenty-three separate blows that they're sure came from that. Then to top it all off, he lit her hair on fire. It was the smoke detector that alerted the hotel staff."

Holy … He's getting more violent each time, Favro thought.

"You there, buddy?" Jacobs asked.

"Yeah, I'm here. He really did rape her?"

"Yeah, he did for sure. The lab is running samples of everything for DNA, including semen, but we're pretty sure of the results."

"Anything else?"

"The chief wants to see you right away … like tonight. He wants to know what leads we have, and he doesn't want to hear them from me. I'm nervous, man. I don't think we have enough. His expectations are huge, and this is my first big case. And I …" He shook his head, then blurted, "I don't want to meet him yet! I think we need a backup plan when we get there. Just start scratching … Tell him you have something. You're sick, and we have to go. Then we'll get the heck out of there."

"Tell him I have something?"

"It'll work. And if it doesn't, I'll vomit. I can vomit on cue. I've been able to since I was a kid. I have a very weak stomach."

"Christ, man! Pull yourself together. Nobody's vomiting. Just calm down."

Favro thought only for a moment about the meeting. It was time. But he still couldn't help thinking, *how'd this boy ever make homicide?*

A bar was the perfect place to meet. They wouldn't be bothered or barely even noticed in such a shitty, hole-in-the-wall joint. The City Lights Lounge. Yes, perfect. He set up the time and place with Jacobs for one hour, so he could drink in peace for a bit.

However, the notion that they wouldn't be noticed didn't last long. As Jacobs and Chief Beckwith made their entrance an hour later, Jacobs misjudged the doorstep, the result being a well-executed and perfect "ten" in the face-plant division. So much for remaining inconspicuous. The chief kept walking, and Favro made no effort to help his partner up off the floor.

"Oh my God, you're such an idiot," Favro muttered, shaking his head.

"It's not my fault! It's the leather on the bottom of these shoes. They're so slippery," he complained.

"Well, why are you wearing those friggin' shoes in here anyway? You're always wearing that damn suit and those friggin' shoes! You look like a goddamned narc! You know those shoes are gonna get us beat up, right?" Favro sniped through his teeth. "You look like an idiot."

"Ladies, ladies ..." Beckwith interjected. "I hate to break up the fashion gab, but do you think we could get down to business?!"

Favro apologized as he shot Jacobs a look. Being cooped up in the motel room was making him cranky, but truth be told, he was just dying for another drink and practically tripped the waitress when she passed by their table.

Beckwith got straight to it. He wanted to see results from this game plan, whatever it was, and he wanted them fast.

"I'm not prepared to take another call from the mayor or read any more police-bashing newspaper articles. I want to hear what you've been working on. So, spill it."

Jacobs started complaining about an upset stomach, and Favro shot him another quick look that said, *Don't you dare!* Then he shifted his chair towards the chief and began feeding him what he hoped would be a satisfying dish, at least for the time being.

"I think I found his trophy, boss. I figured out what he collects from each murder, each crime scene. Cyrus collects newspaper articles and so on about his crimes. *That's* his trophy." Favro motioned for another drink and then continued.

"My guess would be *The D.C. Liberty* and *Washington in Motion* are the two papers he reads, relishing in the incompetence, and even the minute details of the crimes they describe. Along with how badly the police have failed … It's all exhilarating to him. The way I figured this all out is that the letters he's sent us contain verbatim words used in the press, over and over. The police-bashing articles, the ineffectiveness of the force, my own incompetence …

"He loves to point that out, using words from those articles. That's what he's gathering and savoring from each murder. He capitalizes on those degrading words. He's a collector. Other than the victims being female, every homicide was completely different. Most serial killers keep a trophy, a prize … some gift to themselves from each victim. Sometimes it's something that belonged to each person, perhaps something as personal as a lock of hair, or worse, a body part or skin tissue.

"But Cyrus covets current newspaper articles and Posts. To him, it's all a structured game. As soon as the news would point something specific out, I'd get another letter, and we'd have another victim."

Jacobs squirmed around in his chair. Favro was talking way too fast.

The chief stared at him. "You sick or something?"

"No. I just gotta go to the bathroom."

He bolted from his seat.

Great. That's not inconspicuous at all. Jack Favro sighed. He had thought long and hard about his deal with the chief. Beckwith was nervous and breathing down his neck every day. If he had told him from the beginning that they would be in for a really long haul, he never would have gone for this undercover deal. And then there was Dan Jacobs. The poor guy was still in shock from digging up that dead body. He didn't know why, but in some sick way, he found that funny.

As they settled in with their drinks, Favro went on to explain to the chief that he was pretty sure they would receive notice of another missing female ... because Cyrus wasn't a quitter. He would have read the paper, then doubted it. The man was a genius and took nothing at face value. So, he would keep his victim alive until the funeral service was complete and he'd seen Favro's ashes go into the ground on Sunday.

Favro thought a lot about his decision to fake his death. *I hope this was the right thing to do.* Second guessing himself at this point was not good. *This has to throw him off his routine,* he thought. *Cyrus has to believe I'm dead, or we're screwed.* They needed to be able to save this next woman because there *would* be a next woman. He just couldn't let the chief down ... again.

Favro was sure there was still something more to the "You can hear her scream when the bell tolls" clue. Jacobs had told him that the discovered cell phone had rung only that one time, and that nobody had answered it. Of course they hadn't ... because it had been inside of Angela Berg's vagina when it rang. If Cyrus had been ready to carry out his own instructions, he would have kept calling until someone answered.

"... Unless, of course, nobody ever answers the cell," Favro continued, "in which case, we've pissed him off ... He might have freaked out and killed her right away. But I'm willing to bet that's not the case, Chief." Favro leaned back in his chair. He was done.

"That's it? That's all you've got? That's shit! That's nothing!" Beckwith barked. "You still haven't even explained why he's picked *you* as his personal pen-pal!"

"And what's with this fucking table?" the chief bellowed, frustrated by the case and taking it out on its shaking surface. Jacobs, who had slipped back into his seat a few moments earlier, quickly put his hand on his knee to stop it from bouncing. His nerves were so bad that he'd been banging the table with his leg, almost tipping the drinks over at one point.

There was more to tell. Favro knew this setup would be hard on the chief, who was used to getting daily updates on every case. Beckwith had superiors to answer to as well. There must have been some fancy footwork on the chief's part down at the station just to keep things running smoothly.

They stayed at the bar for one more round as Favro and Jacobs did their best to calm the chief's nerves, even though Jacobs's were as bad as the chief's. When it was time to go, Jacobs thought, *how am I the designated driver when I have to keep pulling over to puke?*

What they didn't know was the next day they would all get a big break in the case. Unfortunately, like every other break they'd received, it would come right on the heels of their most recent clue ... too late to solve the puzzle.

CHAPTER 7

THE MORNING SUN came too soon for Favro, even if it was after eleven when he finally opened an eyelid. Every day started the same, regardless of the time: headache, headache, headache. His mouth felt like a track team had run through it. He needed a shower and some alcohol, and it didn't have to be in that order.

He stretched his arms against the shower wall as the water pounded down on his body. The steamy shower brought him great relief. They had a deal, the two of them. It would wake him up, and he would not fall down. Favro didn't visit the gym often, but you would think otherwise looking at his sculpted body. His muscles had definition, his torso an inverted triangle of rippling muscles and equally muscled appendages. If others had realized this, they would have wondered how a guy who beat the shit out of his liver so much could look so good. Then they would think twice about messing with him.

He stepped out of the shower and dried himself off slowly. His tattoos told a story, and he had a lot of them. The skull and crossbones were there to remind him not to drink, but it only haunted him every time he bent his elbow. The floating pearl necklace was for his mom, and the bloody fist was for his father. He ached all over. He always did. Favro's wavy black hair had been shaved high and tight now. His short beard was bristly and untidy. All part of his transition to work undetected on the street. Favro brushed his face and combed his teeth, or something like that. He couldn't think straight. There were mornings when his thought processes were a little slow. He looked at his sorry face in the mirror, and something occurred to him: *Why hasn't that weenie called?*

Barely finishing his thought, his cell started vibrating beside the soap dish. "Christ, that kid gets up before the crickets," he muttered, then answered the phone, griping, "What the hell took you so long?"

"Oh no, I'm not falling for that. You just dragged your sorry butt out of bed, and I know it! All hell's breaking loose down here, and you're just snoozing the day away!" Jacobs sounded almost frantic.

"Simmer down."

"I don't have to simmer down!" Jacobs yelled back into the phone. "I hate that you're always telling me to simmer down! You know … I don't need this shit. I could have been a lawyer."

"So, why aren't you?"

"I failed the bar three times."

Favro started to laugh.

"You don't know anything about me," Jacobs continued. "I got shit going on in my life right now. Jesus, Amy is having my baby any day, and I'm never home. And trying to keep the fact that you're not dead from her is killing me! And after you're done spanking my ass, I gotta go home to her bitching about how I don't appreciate her swollen ankles!"

"Look," Favro said, "just settle the fuck down and tell me what's going on!"

Jacobs took a deep breath. "The station received a missing-person report for a woman by the name of Louise Richards. They haven't locked down all the details yet, but it looks like she may have gone missing the day after they found Angela Berg in the Matriarch Hotel."

I knew it! Favro thought, recalling his conversation with the chief.

Jacobs continued. "The girl's seventy-nine-year-old mother called it in. Every Wednesday at seven p.m., for the last three years, Louise has called her mother. Wednesday came and went without a call. So, the mother calls her at home on Thursday and doesn't get an answer. Now, she's really worried, so she tries her work number. Here is where it gets interesting.

"They say she hasn't shown up for work. In fact, she's been absent for two days and was officially late enough for her Thursday shift to be considered a 'no show' for that day as well."

"Where does she work?" Favro asked.

"Henderson Publishing. She's an assistant copyeditor."

This immediately had Favro's full attention. No letter had come with clues about a copyeditor. The chief would have told him about it. Cyrus had just broken his pattern.

Jacobs went on to explain that Mrs. Richards had been freaking out. The human-resources department at Louise's office had told her that, after a couple of days, they had tried on and off to get an answer at her home but were unsuccessful."

"It took them two days to call her?" Favro said, not believing his ears. "That's pretty brutal."

"Yes, well, that's when Mrs. Richards made the initial call to the station to file the report. There is a notation on the report from the officer who took the call yesterday, saying that while he was empathetic, Louise was a grown woman and if she didn't want to go to work or call her mother, that was her choice. It didn't mean that she was missing."

Favro reacted instantly. "Holy hen shit! We've got women getting *slaughtered* all over D.C.! This dick knows it and doesn't take it seriously?!"

"Look, it doesn't matter because Mom wasn't buying it either," Jacobs continued. "And something major has happened! The old lady went up one side of the officer and down the other. Gave him such a hard time that he agreed to pick up the mom and take her to Louise's house at nine o'clock this morning to investigate. She has an extra key."

Favro glanced up at the clock on the wall. It read 11:22 a.m. "Today is Friday. What did they find?"

Jacobs paused. "Well, interesting that you just used the word 'slaughtered,' because it only gets uglier from here. You see, Mrs. Richards was impatient, and while she was waiting for the officer to arrive at her place this morning to pick her up, she decided to give Louise's cell phone one more try."

Favro's eyes slowly widened as a thought went through his mind: *You can hear her scream when the bell tolls...*

"Mrs. Richards was so delighted to hear the call to her daughter connect after the third ring, but then there was silence on the other end of the line, so she called out her name. That's when she heard cries for help and a bloodcurdling scream. She called out to her daughter over and over, but the line went dead.

"She was hysterical when the police officer arrived at her house. By the time they made it to Louise's doorstep, it was all over. Apparently, it looked like a slaughterhouse. Does the human body really contain that much blood?"

Jacob sighed and shook his head before continuing. "Louise's body was the only one there, hanging like a side of beef from the kitchen fan. And she was, for lack of a better word, empty—"

"Stop!" Favro's imagination had taken over. He took a deep breath and blew it out slowly. This was too much, even for him, and especially before booze or coffee.

"You okay, buddy?"

"Yeah, I'm okay. Can we meet at your place? I'm going a little squirrelly in this motel room."

"Wait ... Let me understand this ... You want to meet with me, at my home, under the same roof as my very pregnant wife? The same wife who doesn't know you're alive or that you're the one keeping me away all hours of the day and night? A woman, I might add, who despite being pregnant, I have no doubt could beat the living shit out of you?"

"Okay, change of plans ... Why don't you meet me at my place after all? That way there's no step for you to slip on with those friggin' shoes. Bring donuts."

"I'll be there in twenty."

Jacobs was excited to meet with his partner. Following his own hunches and leads had proven successful, and he was eager to show Favro his own break in the case. Maybe then he would finally stop calling him a weenie.

What a wonderful sunny day. It took exactly twenty-two minutes from the time Louise first laid eyes on Cyrus for them both to finish their Cobb salads at Murphy's, and for Louise to fall in love. To fall completely in love and abandon all her common sense. She would do anything for Albert named after her father. Anything he asked.

As they strolled along after lunch, his hand found hers, and the beginning of a conquest ensued. She invited him back to her house for tea. After all, she had the whole day off. Her new-found confidence was flourishing. She was practically floating. Filled with love!

Cyrus could barely contain himself. He hardly had to do any work at all. This situation was sad, and he was delighted. She reminded him of the au pair that had cared for him when he was young. So prim and proper, yet she'd beaten the shit out of him daily. He would kill Louise in a special way. He would take his time. A special message to Favro.

As they walked, the breeze whipped Louise's hair around, but she just couldn't let go of Cyrus's hand to collect it. She felt grateful to be tall enough to meet his stride and didn't want to look self-conscious trying to fix her hair. She just kept flipping it around, until finally, he stopped, twisting her wrist a little. It hurt, but she didn't complain. Cyrus faced her directly, and with his left hand, grabbed both of her wrists and pulled them tightly behind her back. Then with his right hand, he ran his fingers through her ash-blonde hair, tucking the left side behind her ear. She froze as her whole body came alive to his touch.

"You have beautiful hair."

"Oh. Oh, thank you so much!" she choked out, her cheeks immediately flushing. He pulled a blue-satin ribbon from the back pocket of his gray worsted trousers. Sexy was the order of the day. Gently letting her go free, he proceeded to tie her hair back into a loose pony.

"That's better," he said. His light-blue linen shirt had two buttons opened at the top, revealing a little chest hair.

Unrecognizable feelings came over her. She wanted to bury her face in his chest, to pull him close to her body. *What is happening to me?* Those trousers hung perfectly on his hips. *He is so sexy!* Of course, there was no speculation as to why he had a silk ribbon at the ready in his back pocket. This could be any girl's fantasy. Any woman's. But it was hers.

He picked up his duffel bag in one hand and proceeded to entwine the fingers of his other hand in hers. They continued their walk, but she had a new skip in her step. She was completely smitten now.

Once back at her house, he could almost taste a juicy steak, rare, as always. He was starving now, and it was time for supper.

She made him tea and put out cookies like a nice little hostess. That's all she knew how to do. Be nice. The whole time, he leaned back against the kitchen counter and stared quizzically at her, one hand on his elbow, the other on his chin, watching her prepare for him, even while he was preparing for her. This caused a small, wicked smile to lift the right corner of his mouth. She kept stealing small peeks at him, nervously shaking the teacups. *Why isn't he saying anything?! Where did my confidence go?*

"I'm … uh … just going to go change out of my dress clothes," she said. "Be right back." Louise shuffled quickly into the bedroom and closed the door, leaving her suitor alone in the kitchen.

Cyrus made haste dosing her tea. He wanted to enter her bedroom, but that wasn't his plan for today, and he always stuck to his plan.

In the bedroom, Louise was firing clothes out of her closet at record speed. She would definitely win this category if there were a competition. *What was I thinking!? I don't have anything casual that's even pretty!* She finally settled on her nicest pair of sweats, and a pale-pink silk camisole, leaving her feet bare. *Thank God I just painted my toes!*

"This is sexy, right?" she mumbled to herself.

When she re-entered the kitchen, Cyrus was in the same spot she'd left him, leaning against the kitchen counter. "May I pour for you?" he asked in his sexiest voice.

She couldn't take her eyes off of his. "P-Please do," she stuttered again, shuffling closer to him.

He didn't ask her how she liked it. He just squeezed the lemon that was on the tray into the cup and brought it to his mouth. His lips shaping a small O, he blew slowly into the china cup. The steam rose over his eyes. She felt faint at the sight. He took a full step forward, and she leaned back, the cheeks of her behind now resting against the kitchen island. His hips pressed against hers. He blew again, then brought the rim of the teacup to rest gently on her lower lip.

"Sip," he whispered.

Louise did as she was told, and swallowed hard.

"Again," he said.

She slowly drank the tea. All of it. Her eyelids fluttered. The room was spinning around her head.

Remembering the "special message to Favro," he was making her wait. Cyrus rested his hands on her hips. She felt unsteady to his touch. He took his time with her. Was it his sensuality or the drugs that made her inhibitions stray? Game on!

He slid his hands up her body, beneath the camisole. As his thumbs grazed her breasts, her nipples came alive to his touch. Her entire body was quivering. *Will he carry me to bed and make love to me? Will we just do it here on the kitchen floor?*

Louise's imagination made her heart quicken as she trembled. She felt drunk. He kissed her softly along the neck, then guiding her arms above her head, he ever so slowly peeled off the pink-silk camisole. *He will carry me to bed!* She was sure of it, feeling totally uninhibited with him now.

He gently tipped her head back and slowly ran his fingers between her shoulder blades and down to the small of her back. As she moaned with anticipation, the blue ribbon came loose from her hair and spiraled down toward her toes. He pressed his hips against hers again, holding her steady, and Louise felt his excitement. She was ready for him now.

Her eyes fluttered shut, and she barely felt the first strike. The chef knife into her right hip. Out it came and into the other! *That* one she felt, and her moans were no longer sensual. A scream came to her throat, but it was quickly stifled with a piece of duct tape, and before she could muster strength or coordination, her hands were pulled tight above her head.

She was dangling from the ceiling fan now and kicking wildly. Her feet were quickly trussed up like the legs of a turkey. Louise felt every slice now, like having surgery without enough anesthetic. She felt it all. As stoned as she was, she felt all of it.

Hanging like a fresh hind of beef, Louise began to bleed out. Before her pulse stopped, he took the life from her with a thrusting strike to the heart, clean through. A quick gasp of air, from both of them, and it was over.

Cyrus walked slowly to the butcher block on the counter and returned the bloody weapon to its allotted slot. Then he stood calmly in front of his conquest. *Looks about right.* He grinned. He stepped onto the living-room rug and made his way to the bathroom, a trail of Louise's blood following him. He stripped out of his clothes without a care in the world about leaving them behind. He took his time cleaning up. He even used her disposable razor to shave. All her pretty little things in her pretty little bathroom with pantyhose and bras draped over the shower bar. So neat and tidy except for the mat he stood on, now soaked in her blood, and the pink towels all stained in red. He put them back neatly on the towel bar. His naked back to the bathroom mirror, Cyrus had the body of an athlete. Trim and fit. His tight six pack would make most women gasp, and some men too, as would the menacing tattoo across his shoulder blades:

Vengeance is Mine
I will repay

If one knew Romans 12:17, they'd know that this would never apply to Cyrus Bircham. But he'd claimed the quotation as his own regardless. He went to his duffel bag in the living room and unzipped it, pulling a few things out. First, a one-gallon milk jug. It was red. It was full of blood. Human blood. Second was the little wooden box he would later leave for Favro, and lastly, his cell phone.

Cyrus's freshly cleansed body knelt down naked where the living-room rug met with the kitchen linoleum. Opening the milk jug, he proceeded to pour the blood out. It swirled and twirled its way across the kitchen floor until it was completely covered. Reaching into his bag once more, he pulled out a navy T-shirt, a dark-gray wool cardigan, tailored gray-cotton dress pants, socks, underwear, and an expensive pair of casual shoes. He took his time getting dressed. Lastly, Cyrus pulled a flask from his bag and a box that held a small vintage brandy snifter. Two ounces would serve him well following his afternoon delight.

He made himself comfortable and waited for the phone to ring one last time. He had done well, and now a rest was in order.

It wasn't until the early morning that Louise's cell rang. He jumped to his feet! It was with her keys on the end table four feet away. One step, and he had it in his grasp. His cell phone recording at the ready, he pressed "Talk" on Louise's cell. Mrs. Richards was calling out for her daughter, calling her name. His face held no emotion as he pressed "Play" on his phone. Screams rang out, blasting Louise's mother on the other line. Then he pressed "End" on both cells. It was over. *You can hear her scream when the bell tolls.*

It was time to go, but not before placing the little coffin he had made for Favro gently under Louise's pillow. Whether Favro was dead or not, Cyrus would stick to his plan. However, he did have one last thought before he left. Turning in the direction of the kitchen, he made his way to the pool of blood on the floor. Slowly bending, he gently placed his hand on top of the immense pond. After the excess blood had dropped off the end of his pinky, he moved toward the side door through which he would make his exit and placed his full hand flat against the wall.

Deliberately leaving his palm print behind brought him tremendous delight. Cyrus arched his back and closed his eyes. Then he tipped his chin toward the heavens, and with a wicked smile, raised his arms in triumph.

And then he was gone.

CHAPTER 8

JACOBS WAS ANXIOUS to talk to Favro. He had just made his first big break in the case. All those extra hours at the station, and all those favors that a rookie had no business asking for, had finally paid off. He had a hit a big one. Cyrus had slipped up, and he'd caught it.

Something the average person doesn't know is that if you are arrested and charged with a crime but not convicted, you can ask to have your mug shot and fingerprints erased. If you're not found responsible for committing the crime in a court of law, you can ask for them to be wiped from the system, say thank you, walk away, and get on with your life ... even if you're a juvenile. It's the law, and they have to do it.

You see, the police, CSI, Interpol, FBI ... they're all in the business of collecting information. So, if you don't ask for it back, it's simply moved from an "active file" to a "dead file." Jacobs had called in a favor from a guy down in AFIS that knew Favro. That fingerprint-analysis system paid off. He had the guy check the quashed juvenile cases—just the heinous crimes, of course—and he'd gotten a hit!

Amongst all those loops, whirls, and points, he'd found a fingerprint match to a young man named Cyrus Bircham. Seemed this fifteen-year-old fellow had liked to torture and kill small animals. Namely all the family pets in the neighborhood. He hadn't been convicted, but nobody had asked for his record to be wiped clean. Not so smart after all. Even though they had already been sure Cyrus was their man's first name, the fingerprints on file had confirmed it, and now they had a last name as well: Bircham. Cyrus Bircham. This was huge!

This was the big break they'd been waiting for. They had now collected fingerprints, semen, hair, saliva, and threads from his clothing. Jacobs couldn't help thinking, *perhaps now we can do some of the hurting for a change!* He felt true jubilation. From the file, he gathered an old address, a picture—a picture!—and his grandmother's name. He was doing the dance of joy … in his slippery shoes.

Meanwhile, Favro had been out casing dive bars and hotel lounges for Cyrus and could have kissed Jacobs when they met to discuss the new evidence.

"Please tell me you checked for a driver's license?"

"First thing, and nada."

"Get the chief to get the 3D printer going right away. Let's see what this guy looks like today. You check out his old address. I'm gonna catch him in a bar, or you're gonna catch him on the street … or in a store that sells suits." He winked at Jacobs. "Let's pray we have time to get his image before my funeral. Arresting him there would be so apropos."

"Oh my God!"

"What?"

"You just used a big word! I'm not really sure you used it correctly, but I'm still super impressed!"

Favro stuck his lower lip out. *Did I just get zinged by the weenie?* And just like that, it happened. Dan was now Jack's friend—secretly, of course.

Favro poured himself a coffee and topped it off with whiskey. Some call this an Irish coffee; he called it breakfast. He had sticky notes everywhere. Those little colored notes looked like crime-scene markers all over his motel room. They had little chicken scratches on them from his meeting with Jacobs. Notes about Angela Berg, Louise Richards, and the murders that had predated them, his profile of Cyrus, his upcoming funeral, and every other thought process he'd had but might forget because he drank too much.

It was all about the game. Was this really a personal vendetta against him? There was no other conclusion to draw. But where had he met this predator? This Cyrus Bircham? When did he piss him off so badly that he'd become a homicidal maniac?

He would need to walk the grid in Louise's house as soon as possible. A whole day had gone by, and now it was Saturday. Jacobs had done his job, bringing him up to date. The crucial time to collect any evidence at a crime scene is the first forty-eight hours. So much for that.

He had to have everything in motion on Sunday by four p.m., which was the time his funeral was slated to start. Almost everyone at the station would be there, making it a perfect opportunity to enter the house. However, this would throw a wrench in his plan to scan the crowd for Cyrus at the funeral. He knew he would be there. Somewhere. He would have to put the chief to work and get as much surveillance footage as possible. During the funeral, he would need at least an hour in Louise's house, undetected.

Favro propped himself up on the couch in his motel room. Nursing his "special" coffee, his thoughts wandered. He had worked vigorously to assemble solid timelines. The evidence was now overwhelming. There was no doubt about it. Cyrus was the one committing every crime. The DNA profiles they had so far proved it, and also that he was definitely working alone. No other fingerprints, no other male DNA. Ever.

He is intelligent and disciplined, Favro thought, running his assessment through his mind for the thousandth time. *He manipulates and controls his victims until he is ready to kill them. He chooses women because of his past, but why are all the homicides so aggressively horrific and each more graphic than the one before?*

Proof was not an issue anymore. Catching him was their problem. He was a nightmare. A re-occurring sadistic nightmare, and time was not on their side. *Why is this case so bloody hard to compute? What is the mystery? Why is he picking on me?*

Favro could appreciate that some murders and mysteries took a while to solve. We now knew who killed JFK, and how Marylin Monroe died, and even that Adolf Hitler had lived well into his nineties in a small town in Montana, only to get caught trying to purchase quarter horses with a Rembrandt. But seriously, how could this case possibly be harder to solve than those had been? In this day and age, even with clues galore, he'd still been unable to catch him.

Favro felt defeated, and he'd never felt that way before, even with the alcohol sliding through his veins. He worked hard that day—his last day above ground. He worked hard, got plastered, and then slept like there was no tomorrow.

It was another rough morning. A headache as usual. With room-darkening blinds, Favro studied his face in the mirror and hardly recognized himself. "*That's harsh. You sure don't look like a cop,*" he grumbled out loud. But then again, he never really had. His hair was buzzed short now, and he had a chopped-up beard. Today was the day "Phillip Caruso" was coming to life, and Favro was being buried.

When he'd first gotten rid of his leather jacket, it had been the hardest thing to do, but he was getting used to the tattered jean jacket now. With this look, he could roam the streets. His clothes had no signature. He looked older and dirty. Now, he could finally go to work.

Nice knowing ya, Jack.

Favro cut the police tape at Louise Richards's side door and easily snuck in. The place looked like a slip and slide. Blood was everywhere: the floor, ceiling, doors, cupboards, counters, drawers, and walls. Two things stood out to him immediately: a perfect bloody handprint on the wall beside the side door that he'd used to enter the house, and the excessive amount of blood. More than one body's worth for sure. He got that familiar feeling in his gut. *Game on.*

CSI had already been there and marked everything and noted the quantity of blood. Even with that pup Jacobs as lead detective, they had done a thorough job. There were colored markers everywhere. He had to be very careful where he stepped and what he touched. It looked like kindergarten fingerpainting day on the counters and cupboards. Had she tried to escape? Had there actually been a fight? *A battle royale,* he decided. The ceiling looked like a red and white Pollock masterpiece.

Favro noticed every psychological message Cyrus had left. Even though he could have easily raped her, he hadn't. He'd left his flask of brandy behind. He'd used her disposable razor to shave. His signature was everywhere. A nice "go fuck yourself" to the police department.

Favro had to think like him now. As he stood there in the stench and spectacle of death, he had to forget about what the lab was processing, forget about the tech guys, the Ident team … The moment they came in, everything they'd brought to the crime scene had contaminated Cyrus's playground. He used his five senses carefully. What had been missed?

They'd had tea. He'd been here for a while. She'd changed her clothes. He'd romanced her. He relaxed after the kill. Where was his message? Favro knew that he would have left one. Whether Cyrus believed he was dead or alive, he wouldn't have taken the chance. Cyrus would leave a message for him. He knew it.

Thinking as he did, it didn't take him long to find it beneath a pillow on the bed: a little rectangular wooden box. "FAVORITE'S TREASURE BOX" had previously been engraved on the lid, but all the letters had been scratched off except the first three: "FAV." The box that previously held chocolates was lined with white satin, and its inside held a little naked doll covered with blood.

The amount of time between the phone call from Mrs. Richards to her daughter and the time they'd arrived at Louise's house had been short. Cyrus would have needed a lot more time to do all this meticulous damage he had done. The size and dimension of the cuts on the body were lethal. The slices were made with specific knowledge of major arteries and organs, and they were struck with a heavy, angry hand. Each withdrawal of the blade had spewed massive amounts of blood, spattering in every direction. She'd completely bled out. She had to have been dead before Mrs. Richards had called. One thing had been obvious to everyone in the field: The blood in the house had come from more than one body. He pulled out his cell to send a text to Jacobs: Game on … we're going to be looking for #6 … Talk to you later. FAV.

CHAPTER 9

PATTIE SAT AT home, dressed for the funeral. A long black sweater that lightly touched the floor, turtle neck and long slim skirt seemed appropriate. A skinny silver belt broke the palette and made her look like a model. Her hands fumbled with the small package in her lap. She had received it Friday by courier. It was clearly Favro's writing. She was dumbfounded. *What would he have possibly sent me?* Evidently something she'd been meant to receive before he died. Obviously, it was a late delivery, making her heart hurt even further. It was racing now. *What could it possibly be?*

He had never given her a thing. All the joking, all those years, and nothing. Until now. Just her name on a package with his writing. Part of her wanted to tear into it like a mad woman. The other part was petrified. She was completely overwhelmed with emotion. It was too much to deal with. *Not ready. Not today.* She shoved it in her bag and headed out the door.

For the funeral, the chief had shut the precinct down for the most part, with only necessary personnel to fill the mandate. And all of this for Cyrus Bircham. Beckwith would put on a good show, and no one would be the wiser. His precinct was still well aware that there was a serial killer on the loose. They just thought the case was being handled by the FBI, and that they would help out only if necessary.

The chief had commissioned a massive hidden-surveillance operation with an outside firm called Your Silent Partner. They had worked with the police department before. He wanted hidden cameras set up both inside and outside the funeral parlor. Not a single person would come or go without saying "Cheese."

Before he'd hired them, he'd done his homework. YSP was an excellent firm. Eleven private detectives would be placed, with precision, up and down the street. Yet, you wouldn't see one of them. Eight more in the funeral parlor were to be posing as grieving friends. There were also two rapid-deployment teams and drones available if needed. They had an arsenal of equipment and spyware and worked on a need-to-know basis. The chief had been getting a little jumpy about the funeral. He'd known they needed good backup and had signed their contract immediately.

As the funeral parlor slowly filled and the time turned to four p.m., the proceedings got underway. People moved uncomfortably in their seats. Of course the air conditioning wasn't working. Why would it? Why would things have to run smoothly today? A precursor of things to come? The chief hoped not. His eyes scanned the crowd and met Jacobs's in the balcony. He slowly shook his head and readjusted his earpiece. He saw Pattie sitting in the family area, and then watched as she moved toward the back of the room. She was headed for the ladies' room. He knew this would be especially hard on her. Favro may not have had any family present, but there were lots of Washington's finest in attendance. The chief had made sure of that.

The wooden pews in the funeral parlor were uncomfortable, and with the air not circulating, it was hot. Pattie had felt uneasy sitting in the family section up front, so she'd moved to the back of the room. The urge to bolt from the service altogether was becoming more prevalent with each passing minute. She reached inside her purse for a tissue to dab her tears, but her fingers met instead with the package that she'd shoved in there earlier.

She pushed it down to the bottom of her purse but quickly changed her mind. *I need to know what this is now.* She made her way to the ladies' room. When it was empty, she pulled out the parcel and started tearing into it. Carefully wrapped in cotton gauze was a small handgun.

What in the name of God?! Her hands trembled as she held the .38 out before her. She heard the bathroom door opening then and shoved it back inside her bag, then read the short note that had been tucked in with the weapon:

Dearest Pattie:

I can't possibly begin to explain,

but should you ever find yourself in a position to use this,

promise me one thing:

Empty it!

I love you.
I always have.
Jack

Her head was spinning. She felt nauseated and needed to sit down. Luckily, she was now in the confines of the bathroom stall. She'd needed the privacy and started weeping softly. Finally, the three words she had always wanted to hear from Favro. But they'd been delivered, along with a gun, after he had died! *Why do I need a gun? What do I do?*

Pattie waited a while longer. Some time to pull herself together and get over the initial shock was in order. *Should I tell the chief?* She decided against it. Favro had said he loved her, and even if this had been delivered with a gun, those words were all she had to hold onto now. She would keep it to herself. She decided that it was his gun, the one he'd carried around his ankle, and he'd wanted her to have it. That was reason enough. She powdered her nose and headed back out to the service. *No more tears today!*

As the padre carried on in front of the crowded parlor, Beckwith couldn't help but feel a little proud of himself. He had done a good job of this. One would think it was the real McCoy, complete with flags at half-mast and officers in full uniform, with white gloves, standing beside the coffin. *Coffin? Wait a minute. Why is there a coffin up there?* His mind started racing. "There's supposed to be an urn up there! I delivered an urn!"

Beckwith slowly stood up, though it felt like his head hit the ceiling as his eyes darted around for Jacobs, whose eyes were already locked on his. He made a motion to the back of the parlor, and they both headed for it.

"There's a coffin up there!" he blurted.

"I'm way ahead of you, Chief," Jacobs said. "You almost blew my earpiece right out of my head. Where's the funeral director?"

"He's standing by the coffin with a big fucking grin on his face!"

"What do you want me to do?"

"I don't care if you have to shoot him. Get him in the back! Now!"

Jacobs beelined to the front of the funeral parlor and managed to discreetly pull the director aside. Once in the back room, Beckwith took over.

"Mr. Yang, exactly what in the hell is going on here? I delivered an urn to your morgue last night with Detective Favro's ashes in it, and I'm staring at a coffin out there. Care to explain?"

The older Asian man was smiling and very accommodating. "Oh, yes Chief Beckwith, I received your note this morning about the mistake. It came with the body. A man came to pick up the urn and bring Detective Favro's body. So sorry, but everything's okay now, and not to worry. The Coffin was sealed."

"Man? What man? What man brought the coffin? What the hell are you talking about? Where's this note?"

It was a good thing he had taken his blood pressure medication that morning. It was also good that Beckwith had his surveillance team on the job in the background because the service was carrying on without him. He needed to get back out there to keep the facade going, but he needed to get a hold of Favro ASAP.

He also needed to get a grip on himself. He was about to go up front and say some kind words about Jack Favro, which were really going to be hard. Either Cyrus was toying with them or another game had just begun. Who or what was inside that coffin?

Mr. Yang reached into his jacket pocket and pulled out an envelope. He handed it to Chief Beckwith. "The man said to give this letter to you after the funeral. I give it to you now."

"Oh, what fresh hell is this?" the chief mumbled, feeling like he couldn't take any more surprises. Grabbing the envelope, he tore into it. As he read, his hand went to his forehead. "Somebody get me a chair."

Favro's inspection of Louise's house might have proved fruitful, giving him lots to share. The chief, however, having just read this new letter, felt like he was having a stroke and did not want to share a damn thing. But he had to, with Favro, as soon as possible. He pulled out his cell and called.

The line trilled in his ear for a moment before Favro picked up. "Chief. How's everything going?"

"Favro. I need to see you privately."

"What's wrong?"

"As soon as this funeral is over, I wanna meet you at the City Lights Lounge. Don't go anywhere else. Go straight there. Do you understand me?"

That had been one serious tone, one Favro had heard before. It was bad. "Okay, I'll be there."

Cyrus stared at the urn on his kitchen table. *Are you in there, Jack Favro?* The tinkling sound it made didn't convince him. *Shouldn't make a sound at all!* It was sealed tight. *Time will tell*, he thought. The cherry wood urn would look nice on his beveled 18th century desk, until he found out. Shaking it once more before he put it in place … Oh no, Mr. Man … you're not getting off this easy.

When Favro arrived at the bar, Beckwith was already sitting at their usual back-corner table, with two shots ready to roll. He looked intense. Favro moved comfortably in plain sight now without looking over his shoulder. His new look was so far removed from the way he used to appear that he had no fear of being discovered.

"What's goin' on, Chief? You look a little freaked out."

"Jesus!" Even the chief was shocked by his appearance. "Jack, I've got something to show you."

"Jack? Now you *really* have me concerned."

"Look, I got a letter a little while ago. It's a major tip in the case. But it's gonna shake you up. I wanted to be with you when you read it, because honestly, I want to support you, but I also want to tell you that I won't let you go off halfcocked either. You're gonna have to remain calm."

"Chief," Favro said quietly, "just let me read the letter."

"Drink your shot," Beckwith said.

Favro downed the whiskey and gently set the glass on the table. "Give it to me."

Beckwith reached into his jacket, pulled out the letter, and set it in Favro's outstretched hand. Then he picked up his own whiskey, leaned back in his chair, and waited. Favro unfolded the piece of paper and started to read.

Jack, if you are alive –

This may shock you. I hope not. You are like a brother to me. I have followed your career all my life. Why did you start drinking, Jack? Was your home life really that bad, your childhood so conflicted, that you were driven to the firewater your father couldn't live without?

Did you have pain, Jack? Do you even know what real pain is? Lovely little home, by the way. Mother that adored you. I would have given anything to have her as my mother. I know your father was mean-spirited, but he was hardly sadistic, was he? Why did you become like the man that hurt her when she loved you so much? I'll pause now while you have a drink from your little hidden stash.

Did you always know you were adopted, Jack? What a favorable outcome for you, to go to such a safe home. So different from your brother.

Did you know you had a brother? Your little brother, Cyrus. That's right. You're my big brother, two years older than me. You unappreciative, smug human being! Do you want to know who adopted little Cyrus, Jack? I went to a haggard millionairess who wanted an heir to carry on her legacy. A little boy she beat relentlessly every single day until she died. With a grandmother who used to pinch and bite him and an au pair who slapped his face for smiling and tried to drown him more often than he can remember. Every day, he ate like a dog from a bowl on the floor.

The house staff in the massive estate he grew up in never knew or saw him because he was locked in two rooms on the farthest side of the manor. He was ten years old before he ever saw a male. Only women. Horrible, sadistic women. He had no idea what love was until he found out about you, learned all about your life and the people that adopted you. Your mother, pouring affection on you, worshipping your every move.

When I found out I was adopted, it was too late, Jack Favro. I would have given anything to trade places with you, to grow up with you if I could have! Like I had any control anyway. But no! You're ungrateful! Such a disappointment to turn out like your alcoholic father, when you had such a lovely mother.

Find me, Brother! Like I found you. Until then, I will continue to kill these women. I will be in control. I will torture them all, each more brutally than the last.

Cheers, Brother.

I am only a breath away,

Cyrus Bircham

    Favro looked up at Chief Beckwith, his mouth agape, his mind a flood of thoughts. Everything was coming together. All the letters, the murders, the crusade for revenge ... Could Favro understand his brother's thought processes enough to catch him now, or had Cyrus messed him up sufficiently to render him useless? Either way, Cyrus was right; he was in control and there was nothing Favro could do about it. More whiskey was in order.

CHAPTER 10

FAVRO'S CELL VIBRATED. It was Jacobs. They brought each other up to speed with the day's events. Jacobs was struck dumb by the letter from Cyrus. He had no words. Favro had drunk himself some more guts and was back in the game.

As it turned out, back at the funeral parlor, the coffin had contained a second fatality. Victim number six, coinciding with Louise's murder and all that extra blood. It made perfect sense now. Favro told Jacobs to secure the coffin, even if he had to sit on it all night. First thing in the morning, he was to order a DNA test of any blood they found in it to cross match with the blood at Louise's house.

As soon as he'd found out there had been a coffin, he'd known there would be a body in it. Cyrus had ignited his sixth sense. Intuition. He wanted a full report the next day.

"Uh, that's pretty fast. I doubt they'll get it done in one day," Jacobs replied.

"Well, ask pretty, and if that doesn't work, slam your fists on some desks! You're a big boy now! No vomiting, just answers."

"Yes, sir!" Jacobs smiled.

The chief was more invested than ever. Cyrus could be right under his nose. If he was, they'd have a picture of him. He was moving faster now. Favro had barely figured out Louise and now there was another dead woman in a coffin at the funeral parlor.

When all was said and done, and the funeral was over, the coffin had been opened. Inside was the body of a ninety-year-old woman, naked, stabbed, and bled out. They knew exactly who she was. The health-alert fob, so conveniently left around her neck, had identified her, and they soon discovered she had been reported missing three days earlier.

Both sides of the family had thought the other had taken her, but it had been Cyrus. Of course the staff at her nursing home would have released her to the kind nephew with the lovely eyes. He'd had all the proper identification and seemed to know her so well. Was this a sick way of paying tribute to Favro's passing? A last hoorah, or perhaps a message: *"I don't think you're dead!"*

Meanwhile, the transformation at Stonebrook Penitentiary was fast and strict. Criminals were shuffled in and out of the Tank, with just enough time passing for the chemicals to clear before the warden was yelling, *"Next!"* The Narcoleptic Sleep Chambers were piling up. Nearly a third of Stonebrook's population had now gone "swimming."

Out of those, eleven convicts had chosen to execute themselves by hitting the black button and then the red, and two had refused to do anything, drowning as a result. Most just hit the black button and were left snoozing their terrified years away. *Not a bad track record so far,* the warden thought. *If I can keep up this pace, all my boys will be sleeping by Christmas!* Ladies were getting a reprieve until the New Year.

But alas, there was a wrench in the warden's plan. The president of the United States wanted everyone convicted of murder in any degree to be tattooed before entering the tank. A minor delay, but a delay, nonetheless. Those who were already asleep would be tattooed before they left the prison. There had been a debate as to where the tattoo would go: the bottom of the foot or the palm of the hand. It was settled: the inside of the ear, so that everyone could see. A quick solution for now, but in a year or so, all the newbies would also have a microchip implant in their heads, just like animals.

"Onward and upward!" Warden Henderson declared. Once his prison was loaded, and proved successful, other states would start their transformation. He was a shoo-in to be director of operations. "To hell with Professor Collier!" he shouted at no one. The position would require a stern, organized professional like himself, not a mad scientist.

Oh, Collier could have his name on a rock somewhere. He didn't care, as long as his own name was in the papers. In the books. As long as his name was in the news, or on the airwaves, that's all he cared about. *Yessiree, onward and upward!*

"Now, how much is that tattoo artist costing me?" he muttered as he scribbled beside the accountant's numbers.

It was late Sunday evening, after the funeral. Time to burn some midnight oil and catch Favro's brother. With strict confidentiality, the chief's YSP guys were setting up all their equipment in Favro's motel room. Even in the confined space, barely a word was spoken. They had the results of Cyrus's juvenile picture from the 3D printer now, aged to present day. The outcome was astonishing. To see what he would look like now was an incredible advantage. Those silver blue eyes.

The solid 3D synthetic version was the best. Oddly enough, the plain head shot was what creeped Beckwith out the most: the bone structure, those eyes. This high-definition identification could not be mistaken for just every man on the street. If it was indeed a likeness of Cyrus, they would *surely* find him now. Not because of Favro's plan, but because of those eyes. Favro felt confident for the first time. For the first time, he had hope of catching this monster. He was tired. So tired.

In the room, Beckwith assigned YSP to scour the perimeter footage while Jacobs and Favro worked on the funeral-parlor feed. It was early Monday morning now, and a lot of strong coffee was in order. There would be no sleep until they'd found the bloody monster.

Favro told Chief Beckwith that Cyrus would be at the funeral, but secretly, he hadn't known for sure. After all, most of his case had been resting on this part of his plan, and Beckwith was furious that YSP and all their crew hadn't spotted him. What the hell kind of firm did he hire? Cyrus had to have been there. *Right? I mean he had to have been.*

YSP was disappointed in themselves. No matter how tedious the job was, they would check every millisecond of footage. The advanced technology in 8K ultra-HD meant zero lost frames. They would view all of it. With all this cyber technology, they would find him.

Favro assessed the room. They were still setting up their computers, gizmos, and gadgets. The things he only saw in movies. *They're gonna need more room*, he thought. The YSP gentleman in charge was moving about the space, pointing his fingers. Favro stepped up and tapped him on the shoulder.

"Excuse me. Could I interrupt momentarily? There's no way in hell you're going to fit all this shit and all the men you need into this room."

"Ah, the brilliant detective in charge. Chief Beckwith says I answer to you now."

"How did you know I was in charge?"

"Your posturing mostly. You're the cock in the hen house. A lot of hens in here. Not a lot of room to roost."

"I'll get you the room next door. You can feed what you need through the wall. Sound good?"

"Food sounds good."

Favro nodded. "I'm on it."

The chief was on edge. There had been a rumor, now confirmed, that the president would mention the homicides in his State of the Union Address. He imagined receiving yet another call from the mayor afterwards. *Oh Lord …* It had been many, many years since D.C. had had such a brutal serial killer running amuck. As it turns out, this president was very good at convincing the American people that they could rest easy when it came to justice. It would be swift. It would be fair. And if properly afforded, it would be harsh.

Oh yeah, I'm gonna get another call. Fuck!

All the tech guys from YSP worked studiously to set up shop. It was a tight fit in Favro's room, so the room beside him had definitely been needed. More money to the motel desk clerk, and a lot more towels.

It looked like some kind of black-ops mission. Maybe in a way it was. The police knew nothing. Same with the FBI. Only Chief Paul Beckwith, Jack Favro, and Dan Jacobs were aware that this was an undercover mission, and that they had faked Favro's death. The other detectives on the team had actually made a little headway on the case, but nothing one could truly sink their teeth into.

A knock at the door signaled Jacobs's arrival with strong coffee and donuts. "My wife thinks you're dead, and she still hates your guts." Amy, Jacobs's wife, had had enough of the case two weeks into it. The sooner her husband was done, the better.

"Yeah, well, I've never been too popular with the female species, so my feelings aren't too hurt."

"Jeepers! This is quite a set up!"

"Jeepers?" Favro mumbled. *What a weenie.*

Favro responded by waving his arm like he was selling something in a showroom. "I can't do this down at the station, so ... next best thing."

"How do you keep the cleaning staff out of here? I mean, don't you think this will draw a little attention?"

"Money talks, buddy. Told the fella I'm a private man with a handshake, a wink, and a wad of cash. Every day when I pick up my clean towels, it buys me more privacy. If anyone comes near here, he'll let me know."

"Sounds like a solid plan."

Knowing what he did now about Cyrus's relationship to Favro, Jacobs tried to step gingerly around him. A wide berth could prevent a swift kick in the ass. He hated when that happened.

Jacobs took his suit jacket off and folded it neatly over the back of a chair. Even with the tedious work ahead of him, he still wore that suit. Favro just shook his head. *Guess it's just part of his make-up.*

"Wow, 3D AFIS! Holographic zip screens! This must be costing a fortune. How is the chief covering it?" Jacobs looked like a child on Christmas morning.

"Well, he's kind of not. He's had stolen evidence and drug money traced back to my real name. A lot of it. Makes it look like I was a dirty cop before I died. No one should find it though, unless they're looking for it, and as for me ... If someone should get nosy, well ... who cares? I'm dead. Hopefully by then we'll have Cyrus, and nobody will be the wiser. I do have full access to the money though. A lot of it. Whoops. Did I say that?"

"Okey Dokey," Jacob said, holding both hands up and slowly backing away. "I don't need to know another thing."

Favro's motel room, though not fancy, did have a nice little kitchen. While the tech guys were filling Jacobs in, Favro made his way to the sink, pouring some of his coffee down the drain. The flour tin held his elixir. He made a fine Irish coffee (in his eyes), *sans* whipped cream. Time was going by fast. The sun was setting. It was time to go to work.

He taped eight by ten likenesses of Cyrus all over the walls. Despite all the technology, he was still old school and liked the hard copies. As they battened down the hatches, so to speak, another war was about to begin.

Favro had a disease. Its name was Alcoholism. The compulsion of the mind and body had overtaken him. He also had another disease. Its name was Cyrus Bircham, which had overtaken him as well. In the tiny confines of his motel room, which one would come after him first? Would the alcohol drive him to insanity? Or the case? Or could he break them both before they broke him? He was already shaky and sweaty. Which compulsion would it be? Time would tell. A very short time. And through all of it, a single thought kept playing over and over in his head: "*Find me, brother … like I found you.*"

As the investigative agency viewed the external footage from the day of the funeral, Favro and Jacobs scoured the surveillance footage of the funeral itself. With only two hours under their belt, Jacobs spotted something.

"Whoa, whoa, go back!" Jacobs exclaimed. "How did we miss this? The navy T-shirt, right behind the pedestal!"

They all questioned themselves. Really? Had he been right there! One row behind the family pews, right behind Pattie before she'd moved. He'd been right there and they'd missed him.

"Can you zoom in?" Jacobs asked.

They squinted at the screen, their mouths hanging open.

"Jesus, that's him," Favro whispered. "What does it say on his cap?"

They zoomed in closer. "Pete's Plumbing Emporium," Jacobs read aloud. "Holy shit! We got him!" Jacobs couldn't hide his joy. They froze the picture and pulled up a holographic image to study and make copies.

"Well, LA-DE-DA!" Favro piped up loudly.

All heads turned his way.

"Would anyone like to tell me just how that son of a bitch made it in there without *anyone* spotting him?!"

Jacobs had seen Favro in a bad way often, but he had never seen him this mad.

"What kind of YSPQRST piece of shit operation are you guys running?! He gets all the way into the parlor, sits his ass down front and center for the afternoon matinee, and *none* of your equipment or men even noticed?!"

Water bottles, chairs, and eight by tens started flying about the room. How do you calm a raging alcoholic? Well, you don't tell him to simmer down unless you want a black eye, that's for sure.

Despite his progress, Jacobs just couldn't help his grave mistakes, and started mumbling quietly. "We did spot him within two hours of—"

"What? What did you say?"

"Nothing," Jacobs said quickly. His place was the door. Everyone felt the same way. It was time to call it a night.

Favro, on the other hand, would be up for a while. He was sticking to lots of black coffee and viewing more footage. He had the shakes going pretty good now. Was it from the caffeine or the lack of booze? He tried hard not to think about it and pried open a window as tiny pearls of sweat beaded up on his forehead.

The next day, Jacobs would pay a little visit to old Pete at his Emporium. Perhaps he could ID Cyrus. Maybe they would be lucky, and he'd have purchased something, and they could even track a current address. They had to start somewhere, and this seemed as good a place as any.

His old address from his juvenile record had been of no help to them. Cyrus's mother had had an enormous estate, but she had passed away, and it had been inherited by a niece. The au pair had supposedly moved to an unknown foreign country. There was no current address. The only tidbit of information they had from his juvie record was that, if he were to show up at the family lawyer's office before noon on his sixteenth birthday, he would inherit $12.8 million, plus incurred interest. He'd showed up. That had been twenty years ago. Thanks to the Privacy Act, the family lawyer's name was not listed.

CHAPTER 11

WITH SO MUCH stress on his shoulders, Jacobs was daydreaming of just a little down time; that's all, just a little. A pair of sweats and a football game. Oh Lord, that sounded good, but there was no way that was going to happen. Amy had stopped texting and was now calling him directly in an attempt to reach him. It was time to face the music at home. It was this case versus his very pregnant wife. He really didn't know which one was more trying on his nerves.

When he arrived home, Amy was sitting on the couch, holding her enormous belly, with her feet propped up on a pillow. She couldn't have looked more menacing if she'd held an axe in her hands. Jacobs set some roses down on the kitchen table and approached gingerly.

"Amy," he said softly.

"Shut up!"

"Amy?" he tried again.

She had no reply but simply lowered her head and rubbed her belly.

"Do your feet hurt? Maybe I could rub them for you, and maybe your back too. Would that be okay?"

"I think you might be trying to sweet-talk me," she answered, the corner of her mouth barely lifting.

"Well, that would depend. Is it working?"

Jacobs was smiling now. Looking at the beautiful woman he'd married, he realized what an ass he'd been. His own exhaustion didn't even compare to what she'd been going through all alone. Knowing he would just be back at it again tomorrow, he made good on his offer. They took a long bath together, and he massaged her from head to toe with her favorite lotion.

As they lay together into the night, he rested his head on her tummy, listening to his daughter dance pirouettes in her belly. Although the night was short, he had pleased her, and he was pleased too.

The next day brought no luck at all. Favro did as he was asked and drove to pick up Jacobs at the Plumbing Emporium. As things often went between the two of them, Jacobs's meeting with Favro could have been a little more pleasant. But then that would break the mold.

When he pulled up to meet him, Jacobs came scooting out of Pete's as fast as he could, jumping into the car and slamming the door.

"Jeez, you almost rolled my car! What's the matter?"

"Nothing. I don't feel well."

"Oh no! You're not gonna vomit, are you?"

"I'm not vomiting! I had some guacamole last night. It disagreed with me."

"What are you doing eating that shit?"

"I'm a vegetarian," Jacobs defended himself.

"Ohhh, listen to this …" Favro complained. "Why can't you eat steak and potatoes like every other red-blooded American? Running around in those Scooby-Doo shoes, getting nauseous, and puking up guacamole."

Suddenly, Jacobs's body emitted a sound, and Favro whipped his head around to glare at him. "What was that!?"

"Nothing."

Favro sniffed a couple times. "What *is* that!?"

"Nothing! Can we go?"

"You just shit your pants!"

"I did not poop my pants! I'm just a little gassy."

"Gassy? You're a weapon of mass destruction! Get out!"

"What?"

"Get out of my car."

"Are you serious?"

"Yes. You and your deadly napalm gas can drive your own car."

Jacobs said nothing. He just got out of Favro's car and slammed the door extra hard, walking with his head hung low. Favro started to pull away, then hit the brake. Backing up, he rolled the passenger window down and yelled, "Get in, you big weenie!"

Jacobs turned around and smiled, shuffling quickly back to the car and getting in. "I knew you wouldn't leave me behind."

"Don't say anything to me. You'll make me wanna change my mind." He sounded tough, but he was grinning inside. They drove along in silence for a while, but it didn't last long.

"By the way, there is no Pete," Jacobs reported. "It's just a made-up name that sounds good with 'plumbing.' They've been giving out free hats for the last two weeks, and report no sightings of Cyrus Bircham. Nobody remembers him. I looked for a washer for my kitchen faucet while I was there. You know how many washers there are to choose from? You actually have to bring the old–"

"Shut up!!" Favro blurted. "If you don't have anything, just say, 'I don't have anything!'"

"Jeez, okay. Little too much coffee?" he mumbled to himself.

Back at the motel, the chief had arrived to view the funeral footage, and Favro was on his last nerve. They saw Cyrus crossing traffic, then entering the funeral parlor. He moved slowly from one pew to the other, nestling in behind Pattie, and then finally making his way to the back of the parlor. Nobody seemed to notice his movements.

"Your Silent Partner are absolutely incompetent," Beckwith could be heard mumbling over and over to himself. Without so much as an "Excuse me, ma'am" or "Pardon me, sir," Cyrus had made himself a nuisance to no one. He'd just waltzed in and made himself comfortable.

"You guys should have spotted him before he got anywhere *near* the funeral parlor! Fuck. *Fuck!* How did he even get past the front doors?!" The chief was absolutely enraged at this point. With all the high-tech recognition work they had done, there was no way Cyrus should have been able to comfortably make it to a seat without being detected. But he sure had, and then some.

The chief continued his rant. "Look at him! Just slouching there in the back pew, watching the Beckwith/Jacobs Show! Oh, I'm sure he was very entertained when he noticed me spotting the coffin. Ohhh, yes … I see he loved every minute of it!"

The head of YSP had just been blasted for a second time. He deserved it and knew it, settling in and taking it on the chin.

Have we blown it? the chief wondered. Had Cyrus believed the funeral was real? They couldn't be sure. Even if he'd taken the urn, which he had obviously done, there would have been nothing to say that the ashes inside did not belong to Jack Favro.

The overhead drone outside had caught him leaving the funeral area in a black van, moving off in the same direction he had come from on foot. But because YSP hadn't registered it as suspicious, they hadn't followed it. Even the CCTV cameras were of no use. Cyrus knew all the blind spots. When Favro investigated the black van, the plates came back as having been stolen two years ago.

As Jacobs suspected, one day wasn't enough time to get any DNA on the blood from the woman found in the coffin. He hated telling that to Favro, even though it was just a formality anyway, as Favro knew it would be a match for the blood found at Louise's house. Surprisingly, so far, he'd gotten away with only one blasting this morning. What a great day he was having, and it was only eleven a.m.

The very next morning, Chief Beckwith woke with a start. The bedroom was warm, and the back of his neck felt clammy. Had he sat up too fast? He didn't feel good. His head was throbbing, so he just sat there on the edge of the bed and dangled his feet. Glancing over his shoulder, he could see that the other side of the bed was empty. Cathy was already gone for the day. She appraised antiques for a living and would never miss an early auction. It was her favorite pastime.

The chief was tired. He couldn't stop yawning, and every time he opened his mouth, his head would throb. It was one of those days he wished he could just go back to bed, but there was so much on his plate. So much to keep track of. He raised his arms to give his eyes a rub and his head a good scratch. His arms felt heavy, and it was then that Beckwith realized just how fatigued he was. The case had become too trying on him.

First things first, coffee. Strong. He grabbed his robe off the bench at the end of the bed and headed into the hall and down the winding staircase. He would brush his teeth after coffee. That's how badly he needed it. Thinking about the house, he knew that it was just too big for them now that the kids were grown. Too many damn stairs. He was sweating when he reached the bottom step. If only Beckwith had thought to brush his teeth before going down that winding staircase, he might have looked in the medicine cabinet. He might have taken some aspirin for his headache. The day ahead might have gone quite differently.

Well, enough lollygagging, Beckwith thought as he finished his toast and coffee and headed back up for a quick shower. He still felt restless. Nausea overcame him as he brushed his teeth.

"Jesus," he said as his toast and coffee revisited him. As he put the toothpaste back, he glanced at the aspirin in the medicine cabinet, and then just closed the door.

"I guess it's gonna be one of those days."

He showered and dressed slowly, his thoughts wandering to the meeting he would have later that morning with Favro and Jacobs. *We have a strong enough case to bring to the D.A., and enough to put Cyrus away, but not without a body … not without Cyrus. If those guys can't find him, what good is any of this?* His thoughts were starting to scatter. Was it time to break his deal with Favro? He decided that he would give them only a little longer. He liked his job and wanted to keep it. Back down the endless stairs, he grabbed his keys off the kitchen counter and headed out the garage door. And that's when it happened…

Squeezing, crushing pain. Sucking air in through his teeth, he immediately went down, missing the last two steps, and falling onto the concrete floor. Chief Paul Beckwith was having a heart attack. A massive heart attack. A bolt of lightning shot down his left arm, as an elephant landed on his chest. Each breath drew in less air. There was no one for him to cry out to, but he couldn't have managed anyway. As he lay there on the cold concrete, only one thing went through his mind: *This fucking case will be the death of me.*

He was right.

CHAPTER 12

CATHY WANTED TO make the call herself. She was his wife, his sweetheart, and she didn't want a spectacle made of his death. The ambulance and first responders had already done their jobs. She had lost her chief. It was time to let the station know that they had lost theirs.

Pattie handled it like a pro on the outside, but on the inside, she was completely falling apart. First Favro, and now the chief. Falling apart would be putting it lightly. It was more like complete devastation.

She felt like her whole world was spiraling out of control. The two people she'd spent the most time with were gone, and what little family she had didn't live in D.C. She had no one to lean on. She was running on automatic.

Assistant Chief Blake Wallace would take charge until a new chief was appointed for their station. Since 2027, every station in the seven districts had their own police chief. Crime rates had skyrocketed after the coronavirus pandemic had left the economy downtrodden and people desperate for money.

Wallace was already in Beckwith's office motioning for her. Pattie rose from her chair and gently patted down her black peplum blouse and matching skirt until she felt composed. As she turned the knob on the office door, she knew everything familiar was about to change.

"Come on in, Pattie. Have a seat."

She knew Wallace well. He had been at their station for three years. She sat in the chair at the desk across from him and felt the tears coming. Pushing her tongue up to the top of her mouth as hard as possible, one single tear rolled down her cheek. Although she'd fought as hard as she could, it had escaped, and her lips quivered slightly. Wallace handed her a tissue without saying a word. She declined it.

"I'm so sorry, Pattie, but we have to deal with this terrible loss in a swift way. I know it's extremely difficult for you. However, I am counting on you to assist me with all the necessary adjustments. As soon as the day shift assembles in the briefing room, gather all the other clerical staff and come in as well. I'll make the formal announcement at that time. Do you have any questions for me?"

Standing tall, she pursed her lips and shook her head. She took a deep breath then and left the office. Her tears were reserved now for the confines of the women's washroom or her pillow. Both would receive an ample supply later that day. She had received her orders for the morning, and briefing was to begin in exactly eleven minutes. This left just enough time to powder her nose, gather her composure, and pray.

As expected, everyone that morning was completely shocked and saddened by the news of Chief Paul Beckwith's passing. But nobody's heart was beating faster than Jacobs's.

Holy shit! Holy shit! Holy shit! His head was spinning with more thoughts than he could control. Jacobs practically sprinted from the briefing room to his car where his weak stomach made a grand appearance in the hedges. Then he drove as fast as he could to Favro's motel. A phone call would just not do in this situation. *Now what?* he thought. *Now what do we do?*

Jacobs pounded on Favro's door as hard and as loudly as he could, and he didn't stop until he heard the lock unlatch. Favro whipped the door open and grabbed Jacobs's jacket with such force that he almost gave him whiplash.

"Are you high?" he asked.

"We are in serious trouble, man!" Jacobs yelled. "The chief … He's dead. He's dead!"

Favro's mouth dropped. "Keep your voice down!" He pulled Jacobs into the tiny bathroom, just out of earshot of the YSP guys. "What happened?"

"He had a heart attack this morning. He's dead, Fav. He's dead!"

"Come on in and sit down. A heart attack for sure? There was no foul play?"

"No, no, nothing suspicious. His wife found him. She said he's been on blood pressure meds for a couple years and was struggling."

Favro brought his hand to his mouth, then down to scrub the whiskers on his chin. His thoughts immediately went to how much pressure the chief had been under.

Jacobs flew off his chair. "This is all over, man. We can't continue without the chief. I'm finished."

Favro stepped in front of him, towering over Jacobs by at least four inches. He was an intimidating figure, especially shirtless as he was now.

"This is in no way over! You and I absolutely have to finish what we've started. The chief wouldn't want it any other way," he lied. "There's no telling what Cyrus will do when this news gets out. We've gotta hit the street. According to our tracking parameters, I've got a pretty good idea where to start looking. There are a few potential bars we haven't checked. We're gonna start there."

"Are you out of your mind? The chief is dead! We have no one to report to! We're all alone here, man. I mean, you're not even a cop anymore!"

Favro was tenacious. There was no way he was stopping now. Especially after the letter from Cyrus. The missing puzzle piece. The reason for all these murders. Cyrus ... his brother.

"Just give me one week. Then you can back out if you want, and I'll go it alone. Please."

Jacobs chewed on his thumbnail ferociously while contemplating Favro's insane request.

"Come on, Jacobs!" Favro pressed. "It's your first homicide case, and look at what you've accomplished all on your own!"

Jacobs stared at him as though his eyes were lasers that he hoped would disintegrate him. No luck. "Five days. That's all I'm giving you. That's it!" Jacobs was firm.

"I'll take it. Thanks. Meet me back here at seven o'clock tonight."

Jacobs was out the door as quickly as he'd arrived, with his stomach begging for an encore. His wife's birthing classes came to mind. He breathed in, breathed out, breathed—Oh, forget it; he still felt sick.

Favro wondered briefly what the night would bring, then dismissed the thought. *Doesn't matter. Game on! That's for sure.* He remembered saying that to himself that first day in the station, right before he'd laid out his whole plan to the chief. Jacobs would be arriving later with more questions than he had answers for. So, he was really in up to his neck about as far as one could go. No turning back. He wouldn't turn back now for anything.

He had the chief's YSP guys packed up and gone within the hour. The phones and earpieces, GPS tracking devices, infrared cameras and sensors, audiovisual holographic zip screens, 3D printer, computers … all gone. Most of it had not even been necessary, let alone used. Even the guy with the AK-47 who'd just sat quietly in the corner and barely gotten up to take a piss was gone.

What a waste of illegal cash, Favro thought. Finally, he could take up his favorite sport again: speed drinking. He rushed to the flour can that held his elixir. It was empty. Had he drank it all, or had someone taken it? Paranoia was a feeling he was deeply familiar with now, like the tremors he had been experiencing lately. And he didn't like it one damn bit.

Ahh, signs of withdrawal, substituting coffee for booze. You just can't quit drinking while trying to catch a serial killer. That had to be written down somewhere. He was certain of it. So, he would continue to make this sacrifice at least until the job was done. No use pondering it further. He would have to make a liquor run.

There were so many things to consider now that he didn't have Paul Beckwith's help. He and the chief hadn't really hated each other. They'd just had a healthy understanding of each other's principles. He wouldn't allow himself a moment to think further until he had a pint in his hand and a forty under his seat. *Well, here we go again. Game on!*

When the news came out about Chief Beckwith's passing, Cyrus could be found at his kitchen table, completely unaffected, legs crossed perfectly at the knee, his posture impeccable. He sat leisurely turning the pages of his newspaper between his outstretched arms, enjoying his cup of Earl Gray and a scone. A wicked smile played on his lips. His job had just gotten easier.

CHAPTER 13

INSIDE OF FIVE days and nights, the two detectives had cased the perimeter of just about every hotel, lounge, and bar where they thought Cyrus might be scoping out a new victim. Jacobs was ready to cash it in, but Favro felt like there was just one more dive that needed their attention: the Lasso & Lace Lounge.

With his new look, Favro was feeling completely comfortable around pitchers of beer, scuffed-up tables, metal chairs, and almost no lighting. It had been a long week, and they were both tired. Jacobs was almost asleep. They had been there almost three hours and were ready to call it a night when Cyrus Bircham sauntered in. Jacobs knocked Favro's elbow so hard that he toppled his drink on the table. Despite this terrible crime, Favro didn't move an inch.

"I see him!" Favro hissed. "Don't stare!"

"What do you want me to do?"

"Just let him relax. Don't stare!"

Even with black-rimmed glasses, Cyrus was immediately recognizable to both detectives. Yes, he was plain, but there was something about him. Favro studied him. *That's my brother?* He knew this was going to get ugly. He knew there was going to be bloodshed. *Tonight is the night.*

From their table in the back-left corner of the bar, the unwavering detectives watched their mark carefully. He didn't make a move for nearly forty minutes. Nursing his scotch on his seat at the end of the bar, Cyrus finally repositioned himself and crossed his legs. Jacobs's inexperienced head ducked for fear of detection, and Favro just shook his slowly. He thought his partner would never learn to blend in as Jacobs pulled this same rookie move several more times.

At one end of the bar sat a rather vocal drunk. A well-known regular named Joseph. He wiped the saliva from his mouth with his ragged coat sleeve and swayed on his stool. His Irish brogue was strong, and slurred, and he belched without shame. Joseph fancied himself in the huge mirror behind the bar, which just happened to display his dream come true: every possible liquor you could imagine.

A big screen TV that ran continuous sports cut away to news about the serial killings in D.C. Several hundred unsubstantiated tips had been called in so far, with no further headway in the case.

Cyrus held the scotch to his lips as the news piece ran. As soon as it was over, he downed the shot. He kept his eyes averted and didn't look at the TV screen once.

Joseph's voice broke in loud and boisterous as he made his proclamation to the patrons at the Lasso & Lace Lounge.

"All serial killers are cowards!"

"Oh my God!" Jacobs blurted. Favro elbowed him in the guts, and he almost puked.

"They come at ya when yer sleepin', or when yer eyes are closed in a sweet bonny daydream," Joseph slurred. "Never look ya in the eye! Cowards! All bloody cowards! Never look ya in the eye!"

Joseph leaned heavily on the barstool then, which disappeared under his rump. His speech was barely understandable from the twelve whiskeys he'd already consumed—six from the bar and six before he'd left home. The bartender looked over at Wendy, who was wearing her scanty Lasso & Lace uniform as she served drinks, and made a hand gesture across his throat. Joseph was cut off.

A voice yelled out from the back of the bar, followed by a round of laughter. "You think you could take that serial killer, Joseph?"

Both Jacobs's and Favro's eyes were wide open now.

Joseph swung around on his stool, nearly falling to the floor. "Ya Goddamned right I could!" he yelled.

And the performance began…

Joseph stood as straight as he possibly could, which wasn't very straight. Then he took his stance, like a sumo wrestler circling his opponent. "First … I'd punch 'im in the throat." He swung, flailing an arm in the air. "Then … I'd punch 'im in the guts." His attempt at an undercut nearly brought him to his knees. "Then I'd kick 'im, and kick 'im, and fuckin' kick 'im. No wastin' me time punchin' 'im when I could just kick the livin' life out of 'im. Ya know, yer legs are seven times stronger than yer arms!" he declared. "I learned that in the army. So, ya damned right I could beat his barge black and blue!"

The patrons were laughing hysterically. Favro glanced over at Jacobs. The only explanation for the look on his face was sheer horror. "Look at the bar," he whispered to his nervous buddy.

Cyrus was peeking over his black-rimmed glasses, which were now locked and loaded on fresh-meat Wendy. She hadn't looked twice at anyone in the bar all night, but she was suddenly flirting her ass off with this hypnotizing stranger.

Apparently, Joseph's performance hadn't bothered either of them in the least.

He touched her hand once. Slowly, his long fingers moved around the rim of his newly filled scotch glass. Cyrus brought his fingertips to his lips, and then with his elbow on the bar, he laid his palm upon his neck and tipped his head slightly to the left. These few seductive moves and a glance over his glasses sent Wendy into a fervor of desire. Favro was witnessing Cyrus's dance of death.

"He's gonna take her," he whispered to Jacobs.

"No doubt. You want me at the front or back? I'm wearing treads, you may have noticed. No slippery shoes," he said proudly.

"Good man. As soon as he moves ... we do."

There was no way they would wait until he was outside with Wendy. Losing another woman was not an option. However, another storm was brewing. Why, oh why couldn't they just go one day unscathed?

Joseph realized that he was cut off, and it didn't go over well. The big bear of a man slammed his fist on the bar, demanding a second opinion regarding his questionable sobriety. Perhaps walking a straight line was in order or some fancy nose touching, both of which he was more than happy to oblige.

Another entertaining performance for his drinking mates ensued, all of which ended in some selective curse words and a helping hand to the street via the backdoor, which slammed on his enormous behind. With the blink of an eye, not only had Joseph made haste of the situation but Cyrus was gone as well!

"Shit! Where did he go?" Favro yelled.

Without a word, Jacobs jumped from his chair and headed for the bar. He ran past it down the hall to the men's washroom. Gun in hand, he booted the door open. It was empty. His back to the wall, he two-stepped to the ladies' washroom and listened for only a moment before booting that door open as well. He pointed his gun. Wendy screamed at the top of her lungs. She was the only one in there. Cyrus was gone.

Joseph staggered his way down the back alley behind The Lasso & Lace. True to form, he belched and farted along his merry way. With his meaty hand against the brick building, he steadied himself to take a piss. His head was reeling as a strong hand fell upon his shoulder, twisting him around and bringing him face to face with Cyrus.

"Hello, Joseph, my friend. I thought perhaps you'd appreciate me looking you straight in the eye before I killed you. We're not all cowards, you know."

Joseph furrowed his brow and stared at Cyrus. With saliva dripping from the corner of his open mouth, he had yet to quite absorb the impact of this statement. What he did absorb was the impact of the razor-sharp knife to his belly, which spilled his intestines out into the alley—the very same knife that was now missing from the bartender's cutting board.

"Freeze!" Favro yelled, his Glock pointed straight at Cyrus's heart.

Favro? he thought. *Is that you?*

Well, what else could he do? He ran. As fast as he could!

Favro fired a shot, just missing him. The bullet hit an abandoned car in the alley, shattering the front windshield. The noise brought Jacobs into view, ducking as he came around the corner. He didn't even stop to talk. Jacobs was now in hot pursuit.

For a brief moment, Favro was taken aback. All the whining and complaining, all the fear and apprehension … He realized that Jacobs had just had enough. He had come suddenly into his own, and Favro was not about to interfere. Either way, he hoped to God that, between the two of them, they could finally take this murderer down.

Dan Jacobs met Cyrus Bircham pace for pace. The parkour battle had begun, off of the garbage bin, onto the truck top, up the fire escape, off the heating duct, onto the top of the building ... with Cyrus laughing all the way. From rooftop to rooftop, they jumped with ease, rolling as they landed. Jacobs showed no fear and was right on the killer's tail. Favro watched from across the street. He could see the next building would be their last jump as there was nowhere else for them to go. This jump was about eight feet, and Cyrus made the distance with ease. Jacobs did not. Favro saw Cyrus pick something up and knew that his buddy was in trouble.

Cyrus now held a high-powered rifle in his hands, a .30-06 to be exact. The detective's vest was rated for handguns, but this rifle's shot would go right through it. Jacobs saw it too and thought quickly. *Don't give him a chance to aim.* As his body took flight, his right toe caught the edge of a solar panel, and spreadeagle in the air, he couldn't land the leap.

As he dropped over the side of the building, his head hit the edge of a top balcony with a horrifying *Crack!* Then his body bounced sideways, hitting some solar panels on the next building, *Smash!* An awful clanging echoed down the alley as his body tumbled and finally got hung up on the fire escape by its left ankle. Jacobs's leg was twisted completely in the wrong direction, and for a long moment, the only sign of life was the sickening moan emerging from his battered lungs. Then his ankle came free, and he tumbled six more stories, bouncing off walls, ducts, and vents on his way to the concrete below. Cyrus watched gleefully from the top of the far building, a sickening smile on his face.

Favro came sprinting around a building on the other side of the street, only to see his partner slam onto the wet sidewalk.

He had seen a lot of terrible things in his life, but this one stopped him in his tracks. This hadn't just happened to his partner. It had happened to the only friend he had. And it was a crushing blow.

He ran towards his fallen partner, slamming his hands down on the hood of a moving car to stop it and hurdling an inconveniently placed parking meter without even breaking pace. A dog barked loudly. Everything seemed to be getting louder.

Favro reached Jacobs with one purpose in mind: *Fix him!* Jacobs's whole body was distorted and bleeding. A pipe had impaled his pelvis, and his head was partially caved in. He had tumbled a full eight stories before coming to rest on the wet and filthy sidewalk. His body felt cold to the touch, though it was still shivering.

Favro had never seen such a look of pain before. Not on anyone. Blood was trickling from every facial orifice, and both arms and legs were in positions they had no business being in. Dropping to his knees, he pulled his partner's limp body up off the ground and cradled it in his arms. It was horrific. Somehow, despite being utterly broken everywhere, Jacobs was trying to speak, but blood took the place of his words.

"I got you, partner," Favro said helplessly. "Don't talk. It's gonna be okay …"

Jacobs tried once more to speak, hissing something through his broken teeth. Favro leaned in, straining hard to hear his friend's final words. As he listened, his eyes widened slightly, then squeezed shut for a long moment. Finally, he pulled back slowly and nodded, setting him gently back down on the ground. He could hear sirens now, getting closer, and lights were coming on in people's windows nearby. Then suddenly, a gunshot rang out. Favro had pulled his Glock out of the back of his pants and put a bullet right through Jacobs's heart.

Cyrus rubbernecked over the side of the building, squinting as hard as he could at the two men below. *Favro? ... Favro? Is that you?* Were his eyes playing tricks on him? *No, it can't be.*

The last thing Favro wanted to do now was leave his friend dead in the street, but he had no choice. He stood and ran. Bolting down the alley, he came face to face with an MPD cruiser that blinded him with its lights, and then tumbled onto its hood, stopping him in his tracks.

A few things went through his head in that moment. The first was pain. The second was the instinctive need to put his hands behind his head, which he quickly did, and the third was the realization that he was about to get real sober real fast.

A lot of yelling ensued as his jacket collar was yanked hard. Then crushing blows began landing between his shoulder blades. Favro was on the ground now with one officer's knee on his back and the other on the side of his face, grinding it into the cement. Then he was being pistol-whipped with his own gun, which had tumbled out onto the ground.

Officers yelling, pulling, punching, and beating him over and over. Guns pointed at him from all angles. His arms tugged behind him, and his wrists clamped into cuffs that were way too tight. He didn't say a word, but he didn't have to. They had plenty to say without his help.

"He killed a cop!"

"Cop killer!"

"This guy's a cop killer!"

Within minutes, there were loads of suit jackets blocking off the crime scene.

Cyrus couldn't believe his eyes. He'd watched with glee as a cop on a mission had hung there by his ankle, then fallen to his death in the alley. The only thing that had bothered him was that, it hadn't been Favro down there after all. Because watching whoever it really was jump on that other cop like a lion on a zebra, and then shoot him ... Well, that just made him want to invite the guy to dinner, whoever he was.

Hmm ... I must find out the identity of my new best friend, he thought. His eyes had obviously been playing tricks on him. He wanted so much for him to have been Favro.

Into the back of the cruiser went Jack Favro, with a final punch to the face for good measure. You just don't kill a cop and come away unscathed. You just don't do it. There was only one thing he could think about now: *Ten years in the tank!*

This was a friggin' nightmare.

CHAPTER 14

NOT THAT HE wasn't familiar with pain, but pain in the back of a police car was a whole new experience. The two police officers had no idea who he was. Favro wondered if they would recognize him even if he wasn't in disguise. *Probably not.*

As they traveled to headquarters, the two officers conversed openly about their cop killer. The veteran in the passenger seat wished it was the old days when he could have had a little alone time with him before checking in at the station. The rookie, who was driving, laughed a little too loudly at his jokes. Nervous? Perhaps. His partner was still hazing him and known to go a tad too far at times.

"You know this will look good for us, catching this guy," the veteran said, spewing his wisdom at the rookie. "All everybody's been reading about is that serial killer and how we've been screwing things up. Now we got a cop killer. That's real news!"

"How is a cop dying good news?"

"Well, we got the guy that killed him. Good news!"

Favro kept his head down and continued working on the cuff lock. He almost had it.

"Pull over on the right, just under that big oak tree," the veteran said, rubbing his five o'clock shadow and working his jaw like a cow chewing its cud.

"Ohh no—"

"Just do it!"

The rookie did as he was told but didn't like it one bit. The car came to a halt slowly, and then they sat there for a minute in silence while it idled.

"Okay, shut the car off, and turn the lights off too."

"What are we doin', man?" Now the rookie was really nervous.

"Just gonna have a little chat with Mr. Dead Man Walkin' back there."

"Oh, jeez! Don't do anything stupid. Please!"

"You just keep your hands on the wheel and your eyes at twelve o'clock."

The veteran got out of the car, straightened his shirt cuffs, pulled his pants up a little, and adjusted the gear around his portly waist. Then looking left and then right, he opened the back door and leaned in. That's when Favro's boot hit him square between the eyes. He flew back and smashed his head against the concrete sidewalk, knocking him out cold.

The rookie didn't know whether to go for his gun or the door handle. Neither was an option as Favro's belt was suddenly wound around his neck and getting tighter. Easy to get to him with both doors open. Favro tugged on the strap, pulling the young officer down hard on the seat, and a moment later, he had the rookie's gun pointed straight at the unconscious veteran's head.

What to do next ...

Well, he decided, since the veteran apparently liked spending time chatting with his prisoners in the back seat, perhaps he would be more comfortable there. Hogtied. Favro proceeded to cuff the rookie's hands at ten and two on the steering wheel, and his ankles to the brake, then crushed his shoulder radio as well as the one in the vehicle. A few elbow smashes to their computer system pretty much destroyed that for good. No one was talking to anybody tonight. Now it was time to turn his attention to the veteran.

Favro pulled the unconscious, out-of-shape dinosaur into the back seat and used two sets of cuffs and the man's own portly belt to present a pretty embarrassing sight whenever he eventually came to.

Hmm ... he thought as he looked at his handiwork. *Boxer briefs with little bow-tied penguins. His buddies will be amused.* There would be no good news tonight.

Favro disappeared back down the lane. Everything was about to change. He sidled his way along, staying close to the trees and shrubbery, until he spotted something he liked very much. A huge, shiny black SUV, parked right across the street. He bolted over to it and smiled from ear to ear as directly behind it was a car that was barely fit to drive, and looked like nobody loved it.

Just his style. This was the one he wanted. He only hoped that it would start. Of course it wasn't locked. Besides him, who would ever want to steal it? It had been converted to electric and had some solar charge left in it. No telling how far it would take him, but there was only one place to go anyway. Favro had no choice now. He had to go to Pattie. This was going to be brutal.

DROWNING IN YOUR SLEEP

Pattie didn't spend a lot of time pampering herself. Pedicures in summer were about the only treat she ever really indulged in. Her long hair was healthy and took care of itself. But as she lay quietly with her "book of the month" on her cozy chaise lounge, the lamp shining on her nails told her that a do-it-yourself manicure was in order.

Maxwell was curled up on her toes, so she scooted him off and decided to root through her nail-polish collection for something to cheer her up. As she stood, her back made a cracking sound, so a few yoga stretches would have to come first. Right in the middle of a downward dog, she heard a noise at the door. It wasn't a knock. Someone was coming in! A rush of adrenaline hit her hard. She scrambled to her feet and headed for the doors to her back deck. She didn't make it.

Before she knew it, a hand was over her mouth, and an arm went completely around her waist, pulling her tightly into a hold she could not escape. Pattie couldn't see her assailant's face and tried desperately to scream but could not, so she bit down hard on his hand. He winced and lost his grip, giving her just enough time to turn around and face her intruder, who put his hands up quickly and backed away.

"Pattie, it's me! Jack! Jack Favro!"

Her legs gave out then, and she dropped right to the ground, pushing herself backwards with her hands and feet as fast as she could go. Her eyes were bulging, her mouth wide open as she cried, "No, no, no!"

"Pattie, you're alright … It's okay. I'm alive."

"Favro?!"

She launched herself at him with everything she had, leaping up and into his arms, her legs had a scissor hold around his waist, she wrapped her arms around him. After a moment, he thought he might have to actually tap out of the chokehold she had on his neck.

"Whoa!" He stumbled backwards, steadying her and gently placing a hand on the back of her neck.

"Calm your breath …" he said softly. "Slow down …"

Pattie finally loosened the mixed-martial arts grip she had on him, her body going limp in his arms, tears flowing freely now. This was not one of her fantasies. This was not a heartbreaking dream. It was genuine. It was her man, standing in her living room, holding her close just like she'd hoped for all those years. It was real. Her big brown eyes gazed up into his.

He wanted to tell her everything, and she wanted to hear it all. But neither was going to happen right now. This moment had just been too long in the making, and they were going to see it through.

Favro slipped his left arm under Pattie's legs, supporting her weight as his intuition brought him straight to her bedroom. Pushing the door open with his broad shoulders, with her feather light in his arms, he carried her to the bed and laid her tenderly on the soft duvet.

One would think that after so many years of unrequited passion, broken furniture might occur but instead … he simply stood over her a moment, taking in the sight of her.

Finally, sitting gently on the bed beside her, he raised his hand to her face and lightly stroked her cheek. She sighed heavily, holding back tears.

"I won't hurt you," he whispered. "I love you, Pattie."

She reached for him, and he didn't hesitate. Favro lowered himself down on top of her with his strong arms and finally, their mouths found each other. She moaned as he softly coaxed her lips apart with his tongue, and then the most passionate of kisses ensued. His fingers moved through her hair, gently tugging the long locks, her scent driving his desire—the slight scent of wildflowers, which he'd savored all those years at the precinct, he was now holding in his arms.

The room was darkening as the evening approached, but they could still see each other fine. And what they couldn't see, they could feel. Favro lifted his leg over Pattie's petite body, straddling her, then pulled his shirt off over his head. The sight of his well-defined muscles made her whimper out loud. Without ever taking her eyes from his, her shyness faded fast. She could feel his erection and moved her hips to meet his. Clothes were coming off quickly now, as she found the zipper of his jeans. Her blouse and tights flew through the air. Her bra and panties and his underwear were now the only things between them and the pure ecstasy they had both dreamed about for years.

Favro leaned forward, taking her hands and pulling her arms up over her head, their fingers entwined, their grip strong as he held her still. Then he traced soft kisses down her throat to her breasts. She gyrated under him, but he restrained her with his arms. *Not yet, my love.*

She couldn't move under his weight. He released one hand to undo her bra, and her teardrop breasts came tumbling out, nipples fully erect to his touch. He took one in his mouth, and his tongue danced with excitement. She couldn't take it any longer and a small love bite to his neck told him that she meant business.

"Whoa!" Favro lifted his head up and smiled. He released her other hand then and pulled her up onto him. She sat in his lap, and they kissed and kissed and touched each other everywhere. They weren't going to have sex. They would make love. He whispered sweet things to her. With her fingertips, she touched his eyelids, his cheeks, then slowly grazed his lips. She rubbed her nails through his scruffy beard and smiled into his eyes. Pattie was feeling emotions she had never felt before. Her entire body was dancing to his touch.

Favro laid her back down on the bed and slipped her white panties off. She tugged at his underwear, which came off easily, revealing his enormous enthusiasm for what lay ahead. He ran his hand down her flat belly to a small powder puff of hair. She was more than ready for him. It was time.

Be gentle. He slowly slipped two fingers inside of her, and the small circular motions of his thumb made Pattie arch her back. His hand moved rhythmically as her panting breaths matched his. She savored each second before climaxing wildly, pulsating around his fingers, and squeezing tightly. She wanted him inside her more than anything in the world.

"I can't," he whispered. "I don't have protection."

"It's fine," she said in a breathy voice. "I can't get pregnant."

"What?"

"Don't talk … Just make love to me. Please."

He believed her but was saddened by her response. He wrapped his arms around her and pulled her as close as he possibly could. He was in love with this woman and didn't ever want to let her go. Pattie wrapped her legs around his waist. She wanted all of him.

Gently at first, he entered her. He wanted to be tender, but it was difficult. She dug her nails into his back, and he pushed harder until he was completely inside her. Deeper and harder, they met each other thrust for thrust. With cries of passion between them, they savored every moment, their kisses deep and sensual.

Favro grabbed Pattie's waist and rolled her over on top of him with ease. His arms were muscular and huge, and she grabbed onto them for support, though she didn't need to. He had full control of her. She straddled him now, and he was raising her up and down, slowly at first, though Pattie's hips were telling him to move faster. In fact, it was her turn to take control, and she sure did. Leaning forward, she grasped the bar at the head of her wrought-iron bedframe and began moving her hips like she was on a dance floor. Sitting up, she tossed her long hair wildly into the air and cast her hands into it, grasping it tightly as she came again, and then he did too. A deep moan escaping.

He pulled her down on top of him then, as beads of sweat formed on her collarbones and on his chest, and they held each other close while their breathing slowly calmed. And that's when it happened …

With an obnoxious crashing sound, Pattie's bed gave way suddenly, leaving them still on the mattress, which was now on the floor. Apparently, her beautiful antique bedframe had had a grievance. They were silent for a moment, both of them in mild shock. They had broken her bed.

"Don't move an inch," Favro cautioned her. And then they both burst into laughter as they laid there, held close in each other's arms until they both drifted off to sleep.

Pattie's white bedroom window frame appeared anemic in comparison to the white chiffon drapes that slightly guarded the morning sun. Sometimes the prodding rays would wake her when her internal alarm clock didn't go off, which wasn't very often, but today was special. She was already very much awake but didn't dare open her eyes. She could feel that she was lying on her right side, and that Favro was facing her. She could feel her left leg swung completely over his body, over his hip, and best of all, she could feel his strong hand on her as he ran his palm (with the gentlest touch) all the way along her hip, down her outer thigh, along her calf, to the sole of her foot, over and over, ever so slowly. But no … she didn't dare to open her eyes.

The incredible passion they had shared the night before was still fresh in her mind. Everything that had happened between them was even more than she had ever dreamed. More than she had ever even fantasized.

He's awake, obviously. What do I do now? How badly she wanted to open one eye and take a peek. His breathing was deep and peaceful. She decided to take the chance and slowly opened her left eye. Favro's eyes were closed, yet he continued to gently stroke her. Both of her eyes were open now. He was lying naked before her in the morning sun, on a mattress that still rested inside its broken frame on the floor. Finally, she could get her first good look at him.

My God … He's exquisite. She actually felt herself blush. *Tough and soft.* Tough in his size and definition, and soft because of the scars. Those made her sad. His skin had all sorts of marks, and scrapes, and scars. Some were new, and some were old. She loved him so much that looking at them made her eyes well up with tears.

She was so focused on studying him that she didn't notice his eyes were now open, or that he was staring back at her. When he lifted his hand from her thigh, it startled her and she flinched a bit.

"It's okay," he said, cupping her cheek, then tenderly whispered those words that she only ever wanted to hear from him and no other human being on earth: "I love you, Pattie."

She tightened her leg, and pulled him closer, then wrapped her arms around his neck. He followed suit and buried his face in her silky hair, inhaling that deep scent of wildflowers once again. Favro would make sure he smelled that every day from now on.

"I love you too, Jack. I always have."

It was a gorgeous morning in the eyes of the two lovers, as Pattie and Favro sat together on her deck, sipping hot coffee on a swing made for two. They stared at one another like things couldn't get any better. But as things often do, they were going to get worse.

Favro took his time explaining his whole undercover plan to Pattie, including how everything had taken shape and why he couldn't tell her about it, as well as how bad it was when the chief had passed away and the horror of losing Jacobs.

"I'll never be the same," he told her, knowing that what he'd had to do for his friend had nearly finished him. When he ended his account, Favro looked up at her. In shock, Pattie's hand was over her mouth as she stood up from the swing and backed away.

"Pattie, I'm sorry. That was too much."

"You killed him," she whispered.

"Yes … It was the only thing he'd ever asked of me. He was already dying, Pattie, a horrendously painful and brutal death … As hard as it was, I know that I would do it again." He was off the swing now and reaching for her.

She backed away. "You saw him hit the ground?" she asked, her voice shaking.

"Yes. And I held him afterwards. It was quick. I—" His voice cut out as he inhaled sharply, his hands flying to his face as the reality of what had happened hit him once again.

Pattie watched her big tough man as he shattered right in front of her. His broad shoulders heaved up and down as he wept—something Jack Favro never did. She watched as he finally let it all out. Instead of pushing it down and having a drink, he let himself cry out loud for probably the first time in his life. He was vulnerable around Pattie. He always had been, but it had also been a while since he'd last spent time with his Tennessee friend. He was completely defenseless.

He was sober.

Pattie went to her man. Wrapping her arms around his neck, she pulled him close. There were no words. There was no need.

CHAPTER 15

FAVRO WAS A good cop, although not infallible. Even his foul-ups seemed to work in his favor, but not all the time. During his sleek getaway from the veteran and rookie, he'd completely forgotten about GPS tracking. It didn't matter what your vehicle might be; if you could drive it, it could be tracked. While his time with Pattie had been way overdue, it was soon to be cut short.

Robert Aldo was a parts dealer who loved his piece of shit car as much as Favro had loved his. It had taken him until late morning to notice it was missing, but Robert was now at a police station having his classic car tracked in real time. Which meant that time was running out for Favro. The man waited patiently for Officer Wallin to call his name.

"We've found your vehicle, Mr. Aldo. I'm sending two cruisers to the address now."

"Can I go get it, please?"

"No, no. We're going to try to apprehend the woman who stole it. When it's safe, and if the car is drivable, then we'll see."

"Did you say 'woman'?"

"Yeah, that shouldn't surprise you, but then you never know for sure. Could be a gang or even just a kid on a joy ride. Don't worry. I'm sure it'll be fine. Just have a seat and I'll let you know in a bit."

"Well, I hope they didn't damage it!" His scrunched eyebrows made his deep concern obvious.

The officer looked down at the details on the vehicle and wondered if anyone could actually do more damage to it than its owner had done himself. Officer Wallin typed the words "TOW VEHICLE" in big letters on the computer. *Oh man, he's gonna freak on me.* It would have to pass a safety before being released. Wallin stretched his neck from side to side, then motioned for Mr. Aldo to step up to the safety glass, which luckily also acted as a spit guard when needed.

Back at Pattie's, Favro had finally regained his composure. He knew that explaining why they couldn't just run off into the sunset together was going to be a daunting task, but once they were settled comfortably back inside the condo, he took a run at it.

"Pattie, I'm still undercover. Everyone thinks I'm dead, and that's for a reason. Right now, I'm Phillip Caruso, of no fixed address. I've still gotta catch this guy, and there is something pretty major I haven't shared with you yet."

She couldn't imagine more shocking news than what she'd learned had taken place in the last twenty-four hours. Clutching her robe at the collar, she grabbed her coffee and headed toward the kitchen island. "Is this going to change things between us?"

"I hope not." He showed her the letter from Cyrus.

"Oh, my word!" she said once she'd finished reading. "Cyrus is your brother? Your *brother?*"

Favro closed his eyes and exhaled slowly through his nose. "He's killed so many women and blamed me for every one of them. He's never gonna stop, Pattie."

"Well ... this is insanity!" So many thoughts were going through her mind that she barely knew where to start. *What is it going to take?* "But he's sure you're dead now, right? I mean, if it's all about getting revenge on you, why would he continue? He has no reason anymore."

"That may not be true. I'm sure that he could make several arguments to the contrary. I have to get him, Pattie, for everything he's done. For the chief and for Jacobs ... I have to get him."

"There's no changing your mind? Even with your love for me?"

"That's not fair. It's *because* I love you ... I wanna be free."

After everything that had taken place, Favro was more determined now than he'd been on that first day in Chief Beckwith's office. He had no desire to capture Cyrus anymore. He was going to kill him.

Maxwell the cat was pining for attention, twirling around Pattie's ankles. She bent to pick him up, and as she stroked him, he hissed at Favro.

Startled, he jumped back. "Guess I had that coming."

"So, you're just leaving?" she asked quietly, her eyes full of tears.

"I'm never leaving you again. I'm just asking you to be a little patient with me. I don't think this will take long."

"Patient ..." She took a deep breath and sighed. "Okay. I suppose I've been patient for nine years already, so what's a little longer?" And then she smiled. "Just promise me you'll be careful. I don't want to see you on the news. I've already been to your funeral once. I don't think I could take it a second time." She twisted her hair around her fingers and looked up at him.

"When am I not careful? When this is all over, I'll take you to Mario's."

"You mean a fancy date?" She raised one eyebrow, looking slightly underwhelmed.

"Okay. Someplace a little swanky, with white tablecloths and candles. How's that?"

"Now we're talking."

"You just have to promise me one thing."

"What?"

"Keep that damn cat away from me!" He grinned at Pattie, then reached out for her. A very romantic kiss was definitely in order. And that's when it happened…

"FREEZE!"

Three cops stood just outside her screen door, Glocks pointed at them as the word echoed up and down her street.

"MPD!" one of the officers said as they all pushed their way inside. "Are you Patricia O'Rourke?"

"Yes," she answered, her voice shaking.

"Get down on your knees!" he ordered.

The officer grabbed her wrists and cuffed them behind her back, while the other two officers cuffed Favro.

"This is just for our protection, sir," the officer said to him. "We're just detaining you. You're not under arrest."

Pattie started crying and begging for answers. "What's going on?"

"You have a stolen vehicle in your driveway, ma'am. Do you want to tell us about it?"

"Oh no …" Favro winced.

"Sir, do you know anything about this?"

Pattie glared at him. *Lie, lie, lie!*

He said nothing.

The younger officer beside Favro moved forward. "I'm gonna check inside the vehicle."

Favro's mind was moving at a hundred miles an hour. Even with the cuffs on, he managed to reach his cell phone in his back pocket and nudged it under the sofa with his knee. Moments later, the young cop returned. His eyes were huge.

"Uh, guys, we've got something big here. I've got this guy's jacket and his ID. Does the name Phillip Caruso ring any bells?"

All eyes turned to Favro.

"The picture matches. We just caught our cop killer."

Suddenly, even though she should have been, Pattie was no big deal to them. Her cuffs were removed. Not taking any chances this time, the cops zip-tied Favro at the ankles and dragged him from the premises like a dead man. It took all three of them to do so, and they could have used help. The last time Favro saw Pattie, she was at the living room window, screaming at the top of her lungs.

After they'd secured him in the cruiser and radioed ahead, a little chit-chatting ensued as the officers stood around outside the car. The officers were making some calls while Favro was sweating it out in the vehicle. They hadn't patted him down. He had been caught, and there wasn't a thing he could do about it. But they hadn't patted him down. It was time to be smart and make a plan for survival. He might be able to fool a couple of people in the dark, or a few cops he barely worked with, but someone at the station would know. Someone would recognize him. Even with a shaved head and scruffy beard, someone there would know him. He was sure. If nothing else, they'd recognize his tattoos.

As the cruiser started moving, he became sure of something else too. They were not moving towards headquarters.

"Where are you taking me?" he demanded.

"To another district," the younger officer smiled.

"Huge mob outside of headquarters wants to see you dead. We can't have that happen before we get a crack at you, now can we?"

Favro found the fledgling's ego amusing, and despite his unfavorable predicament, he couldn't help but smirk. He'd never had much patience for stupid. He also realized that they had leaked some cop-killer information while he was sweating in the cruiser, and that's how their mob had time to form. It probably wasn't even a mob at all. Just a group of their flunkies, waving signs to get some press.

"How do you know they want my head? I've been reading the news like everyone else. Seems all you cops have time to do is screw things up. Haven't been able to catch that serial killer, have you? Maybe it's *your* head they want."

The driver reacted immediately. "You shut your bloody mouth!"

"What's the matter? I thought you guys wanted me to talk." Favro hadn't been read his Miranda rights and decided to lay the groundwork for his new plan. "There's some pretty stinky cheese in Denmark if you ask me," he said, goading them on.

The younger officer whipped around in his seat. "Are you saying you're the serial killer?"

"Are you saying you're a detective?" Favro quipped.

"Shut up!" the other officer said to his partner. "We can't use anything he says."

"Why haven't you read me my rights?!"

Silence settled in the vehicle for the first time, almost peaceful unless you minded the dirty looks.

Two squad cars pulled into the underground parking at the station. Favro was in the first. He began to feel the compulsion. The walls were closing in. The feeling of being trapped for a long time without a drink made him start to sweat even more. Every district worked independently, and although many knew of Jack Favro, few outside of his district had seen much of him. This was because of the way that he worked: solo, silently, and usually under the influence.

Because he was a detective, he knew exactly what was coming. *No booze for a long time. Too late to slip the cuffs.*

A cop as big as him pulled him from the car, his police-issue uniform barely fitting his biceps. No scuffle tonight. With a strong hand to the back of his neck, Favro was firmly escorted into the building. They had every intention of questioning him, but it was the chief of that district that wanted to be the one to read him his rights. He wanted to be the one to look this cop killer in the eyes and say, "You're under arrest."

They met in the holding area. The chief circled him silently with his hands on his hips. He had a look of disgust on his face as he told him his Miranda Rights, stating them by heart. Then he shook his head. "Now, get him out of my face. I'm done."

And it *was* done, two minutes in—with a boot to the back of his knees for good measure. Then it was fingerprinting and mug-shot time. It wasn't until then that they finally frisked Favro. Stupid rookie mistake. Favro couldn't believe it. Back in his heyday, mistakes like that could get you killed. Of course, all they'd found on him were some coins and keys anyway, and no phone.

They were disappointed. A cell phone was always the best place to start. They had been so excited to catch Phillip Caruso that they'd actually forgotten Lesson 101: Frisk him *before* you put him in the car. If they had done that, they might have thought to go back and look for his phone at Pattie's house.

They might have detained Pattie as well. He wondered if they had done that by now. He also had tons of money, of course, but not anywhere they would find it.

As Chief Beckwith had erased Favro's existence from the system, he knew nothing would come up on AFIS or facial recognition. Thank God his tattoos weren't on record. Not a single cop recognized him; even those who couldn't take their eyes off of him had no clue who he really was. *I might actually make it past booking,* he thought.

Next came the ever-popular and thorough body search and health check. Two officers escorted him to a holding cell and told him to strip. With his back to them, he did exactly as he was told, and then stood tall with the palms of his hands covering his genitals. He didn't move a single muscle, and they couldn't take their wide eyes off him. What an intimidating sight. They held their breath as he did what he was told next, squatting and coughing twice, and prayed that he would not give them any trouble. He didn't.

Orange was definitely not Favro's color. It only made him look more menacing. The interrogation room was the next order of business. Favro sat in there for over an hour before the door opened. They kept the room on the cool side and left you in there just long enough to catch a chill. Just long enough to make you uncomfortable. One would think the opposite would be more effective, keeping it hot and making you sweat it out. But no. That just makes you tired and sleepy, and very uncooperative. The cold keeps you awake and causes slight physical pain. Somewhat of a hardship on the body, but nobody's ever argued the case.

Guess they figured a big man like Jack needed an hour, but that didn't bother him in the least as his body had been on fire since they'd first reached the station, and the coolness of the room actually brought him some comfort.

He'd been through hundreds of interrogations. The only difference this time was the chair he was sitting in. The door swung open, and two detectives walked in. One was overweight, tired looking, and reeked of coffee and donuts. The other was tall, clean-cut in a three-piece suit, and slick looking, carrying a file as thick as a porterhouse steak.

Game on, Favro thought. *Game on.*

Slick slammed his file down on the desk. Favro knew immediately that Donuts would be the "good cop."

"I'm Detective Sigler," Donuts said. "And this here is Detective Truth."

Favro burst out laughing. "BAHAHAHAHA!" He just couldn't help himself as he stared the clean-cut detective down. "Oh, that's a riot! Did you guys just make that up? Detective Truth?" He was going to have some fun.

Slick reacted straightaway. "How about capital murder? Does that make you laugh, smartass?!"

And just like that, they had lost control of the interview.

"How about mercy killing?" Favro said. "And he begged me to do it."

The two detectives looked at each other in shock. Detective Truth took a moment to compose himself. He pulled his chair up to the metal desk, straightened out his vest, and sat down.

"Confession? Is that the statement you want to go with today?"

"No," he said. "Will you get me a coffee and a burger?"

"Sure," Donuts replied, too quickly. "Just hang tight for a bit."

Both detectives left Favro alone to stew for a while again, or so they thought, and sent a rookie out to get him a cheeseburger. Coffee was something they had in abundance. Strong, black, shitty coffee. Outside the room, after the two detectives had paced a little and circled around each other a few times, Donuts finally spoke up.

"Well, as long as he's talking, that's something," he said, feeling stupid. "I mean … surely we can pull something more out of this guy."

"I think you should go at him alone," Truth stated as he massaged his clean-cut chin. "He knows he can get under my skin now. I fucked up."

They observed Favro through the camera feed. With his head resting on his arms, it appeared as though his shoulders were rising and falling in rapid succession.

"Is he crying?" Sigler asked of no one in particular.

It certainly appeared so. In the small, cold interrogation room, Favro's one wrist was cuffed to the metal desk, his forehead resting on his arm. Although he was sweating and shaking, his shoulders were actually rising and falling as he tried to contain his hysterical laughter and hide it from the camera. He wasn't doing a good job.

Ohhh, Donuts and Slick would surely have their hands full with him.

CHAPTER 16

IN THE TWENTY minutes it took for Favro's coffee and burger to arrive, he had a new plan in place. Detective Sigler sat beside him and watched as he paced himself, chewing each bite of his cold burger at least twenty times.

Occasionally interrupting to ask a question, Sigler was repeatedly halted as Favro raised his hand to indicate that he wasn't quite finished yet. Chewing slowly, this went on for ten minutes until Favro wasn't sure if Donuts's patience had worn out or if he just wanted the cheeseburger for himself. Either way, it was time.

"Okay, okay, that's enough! You've had your treat. It's time to answer some questions."

"Lawyer."

"What?"

"Lawyer," Favro said as he popped the last piece of the burger in his mouth.

Detective Sigler's jaw dropped. Of course, it wasn't the first time someone had asked for a lawyer. But he couldn't believe he had allowed this guy to run the show for so long.

What the hell's the matter with me? he thought. *I have no game.* He pushed himself away from the table. Standing with both hands on his hips, his enormous belly protruded, with dark hairs threatening their escape between the buttons, and straining the little white fasteners in a high-risk maneuver. Favro tucked his chin in and turned his head sideways for fear of losing an eye. *How does this guy pass the yearly physical?* Donuts needed a break to renew his stinking coffee breath. *I wonder what he did to get stuck on desk duty so long? He sure as heck hasn't been chasing anyone down for a while.* No time for pity. He would have another hour to himself, and a serious phone call to make.

Favro's cell phone rang from under Pattie's couch, sending her flying into the air as she'd had no idea it was there. Scrambling to find it with her anxiety at an all-time high, cushions and trinkets grew wings. They were hurled through the air as she finally laid hands on the phone, pulling it out from under the sofa at the base of her treasured dieffenbachia plant.

"Favro!!" she screamed.

"I'm not deaf," he calmly said to her.

The important thing was for her to stay cool, and Favro prayed that he could make this happen. Nothing could go forward now without her. Hearing her voice was good. She hadn't been detained.

"Sweetie, just take a deep breath and listen very carefully to what I'm about to say. Get a pen and paper?"

She scrambled to her feet and made it to the kitchen island in two steps. Grabbing a notepad and pen, her clerical skills automatically took over. She was ready for dictation.

"Go," she said.

"First of all, look out your window. Is there a van on your front street anywhere?"

She ran to the front door, whipped it open, and stepped out. "No van!" she yelled into the phone.

"Okay, for the love of God, please stop screaming! And *please* tell me you didn't just go outside."

She closed her eyes and bit down on her lip hard. "I'm so sorry. I'll get better at this. I promise."

"Okay. Has a detective contacted you for questioning or asked you to come down to the station?"

"No. Will they?"

"I can't believe they haven't. If they do, just tell them I'm an old flame that showed up on your doorstep yesterday and asked to stay the night. That's all you know. Don't elaborate. Keep it simple. And let them pull those facts from you. Don't offer them up right away. And don't slump in your chair. Keep your elbows on the table and your hands locked under your chin. It shows confidence. Look them in the eye when you talk and speak slowly. Can you do that?"

"Absolutely," she lied. "I won't let you down." *Oh Lord, please don't let them call me,* she thought as she walked back into the condo. "What about you? Where did they take you?"

"The Third District Headquarters, for now. But they'll move me, either tonight or tomorrow, to the Central Detention Facility. It's the weekend so I won't be arraigned until Monday.

"Now," he continued, "this next part is huge, Pattie. You can't blow this, so write it all down. You're going to have to go to the motel I've been living in. I'll give you the address: 2356 Blue Hill Way. It's the Rocky Bottom Motel and Bar, Room 8."

"What?!"

"You can do it, Pattie. Just listen carefully. Write it all down. The sleazy guy in the office will never let you in my room without a password and a payment of a thousand bucks."

"I don't have that kind of cash on hand, Jack."

"It's okay because you're gonna give him my name, the password, and a promise of $5,000 after you leave the room. Just remember, my name is Phillip Caruso, and the password is 'slippery shoes.'"

Pattie was immediately grateful for her shorthand.

Favro took his time giving Pattie every bit of information she would need to aid in his plan. There was one thing he just couldn't get over though: Not only had they left him with the worst cold coffee ever but they had also left him alone with the phone for the whole hour. They just continued to meet his underwhelming expectations. He decided he would change their names to Dumb and Dumber. His prayer now was that the timid woman he knew so well could pull off the dangerous task ahead.

Pattie slipped out through her patio doors. Her usual braided hair was now wound into two tight knots at the top of her head. She looked like a cat but she was dressed like a spy, in the only spy gear she could find: black runners, black hoodie, and navy tights. Just after dusk, she was enroute to Blue Hill Way.

Her EV spoke to her, repeating the same instructions over and over: "You may let go of the steering wheel now … You may let go of the steering wheel now …"

She never heard a thing. Her nerves were so bad, she white-knuckled the wheel from the time she left home until she pulled into the driveway at the Rocky Bottom Motel and Bar. Pattie turned the car off and composed herself, then closed her eyes and spoke out loud: "Don't show, don't tell, don't feel. Be tough!"

She strained her neck to check out every angle through every window of her vehicle. *No van. Okay, here we go.*

She stepped out swiftly and headed straight for the motel office. Opening the screen door made it apparent that there was no need for a bell at the front desk. Her squeaky entrance sounded like two cats fighting. A greasy man stepped out from the back room.

"Hey, baby! For the hour or for the night?"

Oh yes, she thought. This was clearly the "sleazy guy" Favro had been referring to.

"I do need a room," she said, "but only for ten minutes."

"Sorry, sweetheart. I don't have a ten-minute rate. Those business meetings can be done in a car."

Pattie bit her lip and raised her chin. "Actually, I need Phillip Caruso's room. I need to pick up his slippery shoes, and $5,000 for you."

He stared at her for a moment, then quickly fixed his greasy, sleazy combover while grabbing the keys to Favro's room. Within thirty seconds, they were on their way.

"I'll be in the office," he said as they arrived.

It was the first time she noticed that he had a gun in his hand.

"I can't wait," she smiled.

Pattie entered, then froze in her tracks. She couldn't believe Favro had been living here since she'd heard the news of his death. She found her target: the Murphy bed. She pulled it down from the wall and crawled up onto it. She felt the back for loose boards; Favro had told her they wouldn't take long to find, and he was right.

On the far-left side, five boards came out easily. And there it was, exactly as promised: a large black duffel bag.

"How in the heck am I gonna get this thing out of the wall? It's huge!"

Lying on her back, she braced her black running treads on the wall and started yanking on the bag with all her might.

"Come ... on ... you ... bastard!" She yanked and yanked until it finally gave way, busting out the two boards on either side of it and landing on the bed between her legs.

By this time, Pattie's eyes were bulging out of her head. She felt disheveled and beaten. She just lay there, holding onto the duffel bag handles. Then crawling off the bed, she pulled it onto the floor.

"How am I gonna get this thing out to the car?!"

First things first. She unzipped the bag. On top was a gun. Okay. She'd expected that. Then Favro's metal box with every snippet of information he had been collecting on Cyrus— every murder and every thought he'd ever had, apparently. Underneath was something that made Pattie's knees so weak that she sat right down on the floor: more money than she could ever possibly imagine in her lifetime. She rarely ever swore, but today she was breaking a record.

"Holy shit! No wonder this fucking thing is so heavy! I'll never get it to the bloody car!" She put one hand on her forehead and one hand over her mouth. *Oh God ... please forgive me.*

Reaching into the bag, she pulled out a stack of hundreds and took the elastic off. It took a few minutes to count out $5,000, but it didn't even make a dent in the cash. She found a discarded food bag, shoved it in, and put it by the door. Then she grabbed a bunch of clothes for Favro. "Why am I doing this? I can just buy him more!"

Oh, she was on fire now. A woman on a mission. Never in her life had Pattie felt more alive than she did in this moment. She was no longer anxious. She was electrified. BOOM! She kicked open the door and dragged that duffel bag to her car like a firefighter saving a life. She was saving Favro's life now, and nothing was going to get in her way. Once she slammed the trunk closed, she went back for the sleazebag's money. A deal's a deal. He almost looked scared of her. Lying the bag down on his desk, Pattie looked him straight in the eye and pointed the gun from the duffel bag.

"Put your gun on the floor," she said slowly.

He did exactly as he was told, and she stepped forward and kicked it into the far corner of the room.

"Now, you and I are going to go in the back and delete the footage you taped of me tonight. I know Mr. Caruso paid you handsomely to do it every day, and now you are going to do it for me."

"Of course!" He smiled from ear to ear, showing off his brutal need for dental work. Into the back they went, but not before Smiley could grab his bagful of cash. Pattie stood over him while he deleted all the footage.

"Thank you very much. I think we're done here."

"Uh … W-will Mr. Caruso be returning?" he stuttered out.

"No. Your services will no longer be needed. You can have whatever is left in the room," Pattie stated quite professionally.

With that said, she turned on her heel, and although she was walking quite slowly, it felt like she was sprinting back to the car. "I did it! I did it! I did it!"

In through the nose and out through the mouth, she blew excited breaths.

Okay, back home to make the call. Her thoughts were racing. *Oh, please don't let me get pulled over with all this money in the trunk!*

Her fire was burning out, so she decided to let the car do the driving to give her the time to slow her breathing and calm down. She wasn't used to living life on the edge. She wondered how Favro did it every day. Pattie was decidedly much better at taking directions than giving them. Her hands were shaking in her lap.

Soon, she was home and happy to get the duffel bag into her condo and out of sight. Looking at the clock, she realized that it was too late to call Favro now. Wondering if he was still at headquarters or had been moved to the CDF, she knew that she would just have to leave him wondering if her endeavor had been successful. Neither of them would sleep well tonight. Pattie because her nerves were shot and she had no idea what he had in store for her next, and Favro because he couldn't make his next move until he talked to her the following day.

He had indeed been moved to the Central Detention Facility. Besides a blanket, a cotton T-shirt, and a toothbrush, his orange-jumpsuited ass had to sleep on a mattress about as thick as his jacket, which had been taken from him when he was booked. Now he was starting to feel like a real criminal, and he missed his Tennessee friend big time. Guzzling from the fountain in his cell, he felt so dehydrated and tired. No, a good night's sleep would not befriend him. Not on that mattress. Not tonight.

Detective Sergeant Anthony Pucci sat at his desk across the office. He was a supervisor in a task force for cold-case files and watched painfully as Sigler and Truth got tuned up by the lieutenant. His interest in the serial killings was more than a query. It wasn't a cold case. Yet. But it sure had the potential of turning into one. Chewing on his inner cheek, he shook his head from side to side. Something wasn't right.

That cop killer looked familiar to him, and yet he didn't have a record. Absolutely nothing. Pucci had twenty-four years on the force and was certain he had seen that face before. He decided that the next morning would take him to the D.C. jail for a closer look. He would not sleep well tonight either. His early years as a detective on the street told him that he was going to find something of interest. He had never heard of a Phillip Caruso, but that face … He had seen that face before.

CHAPTER 17

FAVRO ROSE WITH a sore back. More than his usual aches and pains. The concrete slab in the detention center made him more appreciative of the worn-out Murphy bed he had been sleeping on at the motel. He needed a shower badly, but he wasn't really looking forward to the group atmosphere. Inmates get hurt in the shower, and not because they slipped. *Keep your back to the wall*, he told himself. *Always*. And then off he went.

There was lots of steam, but he could still laser focus on exactly where every man stood. This would be the fastest shower he ever took. His own menacing stature guaranteed him a certain safety. But of course, one idiot just had to approach—a scrawny, needle-tracked idiot.

"Hey, man! I seen those tattoos before. You're a—"

Before he could finish his sentence, Favro had broken his nose and kicked out most of his top teeth.

"I know you're mute, so just nod your head. You don't know me at all, do you?"

The poor guy could barely lift his head, so he just offered a clear thumbs up.

"Good man," Favro said as he left him on the shower floor, scrambling for his teeth before they disappeared down the open drain.

He'd feared that his tattoos would end up giving him away, but he'd thought it would be a cop that recognized him. This wasn't good. He realized then that he could still be caught at any time. Favro made a mental note: *Only long-sleeved shirts from now on!* Back in his cell, he prayed that Pattie would call him soon. He didn't have to wait long. The guard appeared at his door.

"Phillip Caruso, you got a call. You have three minutes." He handed him the phone and walked away.

"It's regarding my lawyer!" Favro yelled.

"You have five!" the man yelled back.

He hugged the phone to his chest and covered his mouth as he spoke. "Pattie?"

"Fav, I did it! I did it!"

You'd think she'd climbed Mt. Everest. The bravest thing she'd done in her life, and she was clearly happy.

"Holy cow, I can't believe it," Favro whispered into the phone.

"What do you mean?!"

You could have hung an ice-cream pail off Pattie's bottom lip. She was most definitely insulted.

"I didn't mean it *that* way. I'm just relieved and *extremely* proud of you."

"Oh, well then … thank you."

He could tell she was smiling on the other end of the line. But what he had to tell her next would wipe it clean off her face. "Pattie, my hands are tied in here, so I'm still depending on you. I know you didn't expect all this, but neither did I.

You're my partner in this case now, full on. It's just you and me. Can you handle this? Because I need to know now."

He was right. Her smile had disappeared, but if she was going to be his partner in life, it was going to start right now. She was all in. "Like I said before, I won't let you down."

She sounded calmer now, and that made him smile. "That's my girl. Got a pen?"

"Go."

"I need you to call a lawyer for me."

"Done. Do you have one?"

"I know one. You just have to make the call for me 'cause I'm saving all my phone time for you."

She was smiling again. "No problem. What's his name?"

"It's a her. Janine Houston."

"Wait … Houston … As in THE Janine Houston?"

"Yup."

"Does she know you?"

"Nope! But you're gonna convince her to want to … really fast."

"Oh, Jack, I love that you believe in me so much, but I think you've overshot that mark. I'll be lucky to get through to her assistant, let alone her!"

It really made his heart swell when she called him Jack, which she didn't do often. "Pattie, after all these years, have you no faith in me at all?"

She thought carefully for a moment about the night before. Pointing that gun in Sleazebag's face had brought a tingle to her spine. She could do just about anything Jack Favro asked … and do it just fine. "Okay, let's hear it!"

"First of all, keep that money very close to you. We're gonna need every dime."

"You don't have to worry about that. My new mattress may be lumpy, but it's not going anywhere!"

Her devotion continued to impress him, and her achievements made him wonder why she'd never become a cop. Granted, the fact that she was scared of her own shadow didn't bode well. But she had gumption to spare, and that spoke volumes. Favro was so proud of her. He knew now that he could count on her for anything.

"Okay, it's Saturday. All you have to do is reach Janine's voice service and leave your message."

"What message?"

"The one I'm gonna give you now. So, tell me when you're ready."

"I'm ready. Go."

He got straight to the point: "Ms. Houston, this message is from Mr. Phillip Caruso. I'm sure you've heard his name by now. He is being held at the Central Detention Facility. He would like to retain you. Mr. Caruso is going to be arraigned Monday morning, so you don't have a lot of time to think it over. The offer is $500,000 to meet with him as soon as possible, and you can name your fee if you decide to take his case. Please consider this very seriously, but quickly. He doesn't want anyone but you. Thank you for your time and discretion."

Pattie's shorthand had the message down as fast as Favro had dictated it. "Did you just make that up?" She was clearly impressed.

He shrugged. "I've had a while to think about it."

Can this actually work? She felt a little nauseous. It was an awfully big risk to take. She couldn't help but worry. There was no backup plan. "Five hundred thousand dollars. That's a lot of money, Favro."

"Well, her usual retainer is $350K, so actually, I might not be offering enough."

"Oh, my Lord! What if she doesn't get the message? It's just her voice service!"

"Oh, she'll get it. This woman does not miss a call."

Right on time, the guard showed up to retrieve the phone. Favro handed it over with a smile, and no words were exchanged.

Here we go again. Game on.

Right about the time Detective Sergeant Anthony Pucci had his arms stretched out in front of him as he passed through security at the detention facility, another man was stretching his arms out as well. Cyrus Bircham was holding out *The D.C. Liberty* and devouring the front-page headline: COP KILLER IN CUSTODY!

"My new best friend …" Cyrus said out loud with a smile. "Not supposed to get caught, you naughty boy!" He hesitated a moment as he read further. "Wait … What's this? Hey! He didn't beat the guy up!" he shouted loudly. "I saw everything, stupid reporter!"

His jaw clenched tighter and tighter as he read the article to the end. He crumpled the paper. "I'm gonna kill your mother, or your wife! Stupid reporter!"

He set the paper down on the kitchen table and shook his head, then reached for his scissors. Just because the article wasn't about him didn't mean he shouldn't add it to his personal shrine. A new shrine, all about his new friend.

"Phillip Caruso … Not supposed to get caught!"

As Favro laid on his bare mattress, he could hear footsteps coming down the corridor. Pucci was approaching his cell with a purpose.

"Excuse me, Mr. Caruso? I was wondering if we could have a word?"

He recognized the voice immediately but didn't move an inch. "I wasn't expecting any visitors."

"Perhaps you'd make an exception for an old friend?"

Pucci stood his ground, and Favro kept his composure. "I don't know you."

"Well, you haven't looked at me, so how do you know that's true?"

"I don't have any friends."

"I can assure you, I'm a friend."

Favro pondered his next move carefully. He rose from his feeble bed and moved to the bars of his cell, then squared himself up to the familiar man. They stared at one another for a moment. Favro narrowed his eyes.

Pucci spoke first. "My mistake. I thought I knew you."

He stuck his hand through the bars. Favro left him hanging and responded in his most intimidating voice.

"I said I don't have any friends."

Pucci nodded, still holding his gaze. "I believe you."

The detective sergeant turned and walked away, recalling the first time he'd met Jack Favro. Not quite twenty years earlier, the young officer had been asked to tag along while Pucci interrogated a witness in the hospital regarding a cold case. Favro had maybe said three words the entire time they'd been in the ER, though Pucci would soon learn that Favro was more a man of action.

They'd been in the parkade, making their twirling circles down to the exit, approaching their turn to leave. When Pucci had rolled down his window to scan his pass card, an enormous forearm, holding a twelve-inch butcher's knife, had thrust its way through the car window, right under his nose.

"Game on!" Favro had shouted—the first loud and clear words Favro had uttered all evening. Pucci's first instinct had been to lean back, but Favro had leaned in. He'd reached across the driver's seat, grabbed the hairy wrist with one hand, and pressed the power-window button with the other. Then he'd yanked as hard as he could, capturing their assailant, who was now stuck with nowhere to go and dropped the butcher knife right in Pucci's lap.

The man was inside the car up to his shoulder, and before the detective could say or do anything, Favro had been out the door, around the car, and putting his boots to the guy, breaking his ankle and leaving him hanging from the window. Then he'd come around, gotten back in the passenger side, and said, "Well? What are you waiting for? Open your window."

Pucci couldn't believe it, but he'd done as he was told. He'd quickly swiped his pass, raising the guard pole, and they'd driven off, leaving the guy there on the ground, crying like a baby. Favro had picked up the knife off of Pucci's lap, telling him that he didn't have one like it and had decided he would keep it. They'd never spoken about it. No report. Nothing. Pucci knew that night that Favro would never like working with a partner. Strong silent type. And it would be four years before he'd ever have the pleasure again.

A summer night. Some of the guys blowing off steam in a bar after work. The senior officer noticed Jack having a few too many, so he decided to keep an eye on him. Oblivious to this, Jack downed his eighth shot and decided to call it a night. And that's when it happened …

As Favro reached the door, a foul-smelling man decided to help him on his way. And as things usually went, the haymakers started flying. Everyone jumped in. It was like the Wild West, cops and robbers, good guys and bad guys. Who was who? At some point in the scrimmage, a long two by two with a nail in the end made its entrance.

Pucci jumped in to defend Favro, but it quickly became the other way around. As the homemade weapon swung at Pucci's head, Favro jumped in front of it, and then the fight continued with the board and nail embedded in Jack's left shoulder blade. He barely noticed. It just hung there while he continued to waylay his resentments on "El Stinko," the person who'd pissed him off in the first place. Twelve minutes later, everyone was covered with blood, and the supposed good guys had the bad guys in cuffs.

Favro had never even known that Pucci was there. He was comfortably anesthetized with the board and nail still stuck in his shoulder blade.

CHAPTER 18

MONDAY MORNING, 9:15. Jack Favro appeared before Judge Halliday for his arraignment. Standing next to him was Janine Houston. To the left of them was U.S. Assistant Prosecuting Attorney for the District of Columbia, William Salter.

Janine Houston was a criminal-defense attorney. But more than that, she had a specialty: violent crimes. Since crossing the line from prosecutor to defense, she hadn't lost a case. That was eight years ago.

Judge Halliday had a no-nonsense reputation with eighteen years on the bench and awards for distinguished service and leadership excellence. The match had begun.

The court clerk approached the bench. "Docket number 95378. People v. Phillip Caruso. Charges are murder in the second degree and felonious assault under heinous circumstances."

Judge Halliday sorted some papers at the bench. Then with a quick glance to the two parties in front of him, he got straight down to business.

"Good morning, everybody. I trust we're all in order today. I have a ten o'clock pickleball match. I don't want to be late."

"Good morning, Your Honor. The People are ready."

"Your Honor, Counsel is ready."

"Ms. Houston, pleasure to see you again. It's been a minute."

"Yes, your Honor. Three hundred twenty-seven days."

The judge smiled. Her reply didn't surprise him in the least. "Nice to be remembered. How does your client plead?"

Favro spoke clearly. "Not guilty."

"People on bail?"

"Your Honor, Mr. Caruso brutally battered one of our own D.C. detectives, and then murdered him in the street."

The judge nodded. *"Ahh,* heinous circumstances."

"He's also of no known address and poses a flight risk. We ask for remand. No bail."

Janine's response was quick but calm. "First of all, Your Honor, *alleged* murder. We plan to show that Mr. Caruso did *not* murder Detective Dan Jacobs, as accused, but was acting on a dying declaration, and secondly, that the People have no evidence that Detective Jacobs was beaten."

Mr. Salter was a little more ardent. "Are you kidding me? Have you seen the photos? Your Honor, this is the first I've heard of this 'dying declaration.' It's ridiculous! Mr. Caruso shot Dan Jacobs with an unregistered weapon and assaulted him!"

"Excuse me, Judge, but are we trying this case now?" Janine was composed but made her point clear. "What he's saying is completely unfounded, and furthermore, at this time, my client would like to waive his right to a jury trial, and we'd like to make a motion for a bench trial."

"What?" The prosecution looked completely shocked, and the judge pounded his gavel.

"Okay, everybody, just grab your britches! First of all, on bail, I'm inclined to side with the People, Ms. Houston."

"Your Honor, my client is not homeless. He is staying with a friend who worked for the recently deceased Police Chief Paul Beckwith for more than twelve years and is still employed with the department headquarters. She's very credible. We ask for bail in the amount of $100,000."

"Mr. Salter?"

"Well, why don't we just call it Christmas, and everybody gets a car!" Salter was twisting and waving his arms around like a mad man. He had just lost his lead with the judge.

Halliday was quick to respond. "Do the People need a moment to medicate?" Judge Halliday despised yelling in his courtroom, unless he was the one doing it. "A little hint, Counselor? This is not the way to my heart."

Salter took a moment to straighten his jacket collar and take a sip of water. "My apologies to the Court. Does Mr. Caruso have a job?"

"Ms. Houston?"

"Not at this time. Obviously, these charges would impede his ability to be gainfully employed."

Salter responded. "The People ask for three million dollars bail."

Janine was up to bat, and her syrupy smile was aimed directly at Judge Halliday. "Now, Your Honor, where would a Good Samaritan and average citizen like Mr. Caruso come up with that kind of money?"

"The Court appreciates your effort, Ms. Houston. Bail is set at one million, cash or bond, and he will surrender his passport.

"Now," he continued, "regarding the Bench trial. For a murder case? Ms. Houston, really? Have you discussed with your client the risks of waiving a jury trial?"

"I have, Your Honor."

Judge Halliday turned his sights on Favro. "Mr. Caruso, a few questions … Are you under the influence of any alcohol or drugs of any kind today?"

"No, Your Honor."

"Have you been promised anything for giving up your right to a jury trial?"

"No, Your Honor."

"Have you been threatened, pressured, or forced in any way to give up your right to a jury trial?"

"No, Your Honor."

"Do you fully understand the risks and consequences? And that the judge's decision is final?"

Favro knew he was betting everything on his next few words—and betting big on Janine Houston. "Yes, Your Honor. I do."

The judge took a deep breath and exhaled loudly. "Mr. Salter, what do you think?"

"Well, given that you're actually considering this, Your Honor, I'd like a while to think about it."

"And in a perfect world, I'd make it to my pickleball match on time, but we don't always get what we want. You think you have a strong case?"

"Of course I do!" Salter said, sounding insulted.

"Well, then Mr. Caruso has a right to a speedy trial. Let's give it to him. Motion is accepted. Bench trial granted. Court date, six weeks from today."

"Six weeks, Your Honor!? That's hardly enough time to prepare for a homicide Bench trial. I'll need twelve to sixteen minimum."

"Speedy trial, Counselor. If you need a continuance, put a motion in with the judge you pull for trial. Any other squabbles for today?"

Salter's scrunched brow was indicative of the scornful abuse he had suffered in court and would share with his wife and uninterested kids over dinner later that day.

Janine just smiled and threw her hands up, but the judge was unimpressed. "Don't look so happy, Ms. Houston. You've got your plate full."

Judge Halliday banged the wooden extension of his arm, and then it was over. A guard sidled up to Favro, and he was escorted out of the courtroom, but not before Janine had a chance to whisper, "You'll see me soon. Money, money, money."

Favro wasn't going to fool around with a bail bondsman's 10 percent. Once he arrived back at the detention facility, he contacted Pattie and arranged for her to bail him out with the full one million in cash. He was out on the street in thirty minutes. No more slow and steady. Being locked up grated on his every nerve. Being controlled was not his thing.

All his hard work and his plan to catch Cyrus was becoming a long-running nightmare with no ending. He was failing big time. His ego was going to get more people killed, and he knew it.

As he sat in Pattie's condo kitchen in The Thinker position, he decided: It was time. Pattie could tell by the look on his face that the next thing out of his mouth was going to be of great significance. He had a look of defeat on his face. Exhausted defeat. She had never seen that before.

"What are you thinking, Jack?"

"I'm thinking I don't want this trial to go sideways and end up in the Tank for ten years. And I'm thinking I can't let Cyrus continue killing women just because I need to be the one to catch him. So, I'm gonna call Janine, and you and I are gonna meet her and spill the beans. *All* the beans. Tell her who I really am. Then we'll call Chief Wallace, tell him, and then go to the U.S. attorney and tell her everything too. And if I'm not back in jail by then, we're going to bring the entire D.C. police force down on Cyrus Bircham's ass and catch that son of a bitch once and for all. It's over, Pattie. We have enough to find him now. I just can't do it alone, and it's time to admit that. So, let's do it … now."

Pattie let out the biggest sigh of relief. She hung her head, and then went to her man, wrapping her arms around him.

"You said you wouldn't leave me, so when we talk to the U.S. attorney, we are going to cut some kind of deal to make sure you don't do any jail time. Do you understand me?"

He smiled at her. She was his true partner in this, assertive and serious. He wasn't sure the U.S. attorney would give him any deal. Karen Davis was pretty tough, and it had just occurred to him that she might charge Pattie with obstruction of justice. *Might have to cut a deal for her too. Poor Pattie*, he thought. *I really messed this up.*

Pattie made Favro a strong cup of coffee while he made himself comfortable on her couch to call Janine, who picked up on the second ring.

"Well, that was fast," she said.

"You taking your own calls now?" He hadn't lost his sarcasm.

"I knew it was you. Why keep up the formalities when you've paid me so much to be your friend."

"Ouch! That hurts," Favro pouted.

"Come on, you've got bigger shoulders than that." He could tell that she was smiling.

"Look, Janine, I need to see you."

"Not thinking of running, are you?"

"No, no. Just the opposite. But prepare yourself for a shock."

"Nothing shocks me. I'm as cool as an ice cube. When do you want to see me?"

"Now would be good. At your office."

"Hell no. My office is bugged."

"You know this and let it go on?!" Favro was shocked.

"Of course. It's how I win half my cases. We're talking on my cell right now, way out of range."

"Alrighty then. Gotcha."

He didn't really though. Favro didn't know much about defending criminal law—what you could and couldn't get away with, legally or illegally—so he didn't ask anything else.

"There's a sandwich shop called Lita's on Dupont Circle. How about an hour from now?"

"Perfect! A late business lunch. I'm starving. I'll add it to your bill."

This woman was as cool as they come. She'd have to be on fire for her blood pressure to rise, which would probably explain why she was the most sought-after defense attorney in Washington D.C., Maryland, and Virginia. The prosecution could never get a rise out of her, yet at the drop of a dime, she could have a jury empathizing and eating right out of her hands. There was a rumor that she had an IQ of 160. That's intimidatingly high. Scary high. Even if it wasn't true, the rumor would be enough to give most prosecutors sailor legs before a trial.

"Okay, Pattie, you're up. You gotta call Blake Wallace. You've got his direct line, right?"

Wallace wasn't an assistant anymore. He'd made full chief, and she worked directly for him. He liked her, but she wasn't sure he'd drop everything to meet her. She'd have to have an excellent reason.

"How long do you think we'll need with Janine?"

"I don't know, an hour maybe."

"Give me a minute. I want to make this call from the bedroom."

She grabbed her cell from the kitchen island and walked right out of the room. Favro was a little taken aback, and a little nervous. But given all the times he'd asked her to trust him, he guessed he could afford her this courtesy without question.

The chief's phone line trilled, and he answered it quickly. "Chief Wallace here ... Pattie! What are you doing calling me on your day off? ... Excuse me? ... What are you talking about? ... Just take it easy ... Don't you do that! I'll be on time. I'll come alone. I promise."

When Pattie came out of the bedroom, Favro was standing and staring at her. His hands flew up. "Well?"

She smiled and fluttered her eyelashes. "We should leave now."

He smiled a little smile, and then they were out the door.

Another problem was brewing. The fact that Phillip Caruso had made bail so quickly, and paid one million cash to do so, didn't take long to hit the airwaves. This was national news, and Cyrus was very interested in what his new best friend was up to. How in the world did this cop-killing street person have a million dollars to make bail? This was a question he wanted an answer to. It was time to become acquainted. Every cop in D.C. knew where Mr. Caruso was, so it wouldn't take long to find him. He did his best work at night though, so a little nap was in order first. Followed by some Earl Gray and a little detective work of his own.

CHAPTER 19

LITA'S SANDWICH SHOP was busy, but they were still able to find a booth that was private enough to talk. Pattie and Favro had barely arrived when Janine came walking through the door. She was all smiles, and Favro couldn't help wondering how she'd handle this bombshell of information. She slid onto the bench across from him. And as usual, he thought to himself ... *Game on.*

"Okay, kids, what's the scoop? Time is your money, as I always say." Her sarcasm was worse than his.

"Get your pad and pen ready," he ordered.

Janine responded with a simple "Okay," but her face displayed another response.

Favro opened his mouth and began simply. "My name is not Phillip Caruso ..." And then he didn't stop talking for another twenty-five minutes. All the while, Janine wrote feverishly on her yellow pad, stopping once in a while to rub her forehead with the back of her hand.

When he was done, he took a deep breath and let it out slowly.

Janine set her pen down on the yellow pad for the first time since he'd started talking. She sat back and pondered him for a moment. Favro was thinking that she didn't *look* mad, but it *was* the first time he had seen her appear anxious.

"You couldn't tell me this *before* we went to court, hmm? We're in a shitstorm now! Tell me what you want to do before I tell you what you *should* do."

And just like that, she had composed herself. She hadn't run away, so that was a good sign. Of course, the fact that he had used her could also implicate her. This was not good, and Janine knew it.

"Oh, Lordie, I am going to charge you so much money to keep you out of jail … because apparently I'm going to have to keep *myself* out too."

Favro sighed again. "I think I need to break my cover now and come forward with the truth. Too much has happened. It's out of my control."

"You're right about that," she said, quick to agree. "Now, let me tell you what *I* think. I'll meet with the U.S. attorney, and you meet with Chief Wallace. We tell them exactly what you told me. I'll protect you and Pattie from prosecution. There will be enough evidence that Chief Beckwith okayed this operation. But one thing stays the same for right now: You are Phillip Caruso until Cyrus Bircham is caught. You may need to go into hiding for a while. Cyrus might figure out who you really are, and you're not very popular with the public or any D.C. cop right now either."

Favro nodded his head. Far be it for him to not take her advice. She was in charge now.

Pattie spoke up for the first time. "Chief Wallace is on his way here. So that part of your plan is already in motion. We were gonna tell the both of you everything, so I guess we did something right."

Janine winked at Favro. "Hang onto this one. She's good for you."

He smiled. "That's the best advice you've given me so far."

"You know I'm gonna have to wear hockey gear when I meet with Karen Davis. She's gonna kill me. I'll talk to you tomorrow."

As quickly as she'd arrived, she was gone. Judge Halliday had been right that day in court when he'd told her she had a lot on her plate. She had a lot to prepare before meeting with the U.S. attorney. Thank God they knew each other. Karen Davis was tough; she wouldn't have the job she did if she wasn't. They'd first met in law school, but truthfully, it was their mothers who knew each other best. Something in common to break the ice for what was going to be an extremely unpleasant conversation.

Next up, Chief Wallace. Exactly ten minutes after Janine left, he was walking through the door. His eyes caught Pattie's, and he made a beeline straight to her. "What's going on, Pattie? What is this?"

"Thanks for coming, Chief. Please sit down."

"I'm not doing anything until you tell me what's going on. I mean ... you call me, frantic and saying you're depressed and going to hurt yourself, and yet here you are and—"

"Sit down!" Her voice was demanding, and this time he did as he was told. "Take a good look at this man beside me. Who do you see?"

"I see a cop killer that you're harboring for God only knows what reason. And I can only imagine that you're having some kind of mental breakdown."

She decided that a slightly gentler approach might work. In a calmer, quieter voice, she spoke again. "Chief, look really close. He doesn't look familiar at all?"

Favro squeezed Pattie's hand. "I think I should take over from here ... My name is Favro, Detective Jack Favro."

"What?" Wallace leaned in, his brow furrowing for a moment before smoothing back out as his eyes widened. Although he'd been assistant chief for a while, he hadn't worked with Favro for some time.

"Oh my God! It *is* you! You're alive! Wait ... What? How are you alive? What are you two up to?"

Favro put his hand up. "I'm going to tell you everything, right now. Just please hear me out before you do anything ... for Pattie's sake. Okay?"

The chief leaned back and put his hand to his chin. "I'm listening."

And Favro began once again. "My death, the funeral ... everything about it was faked so I could work undercover."

"As what?!" Wallace snapped.

"Patience, please!" he continued. "Not *as* anything. I was tracking our serial killer, Cyrus Bircham, with the help of Chief Beckwith and Dan Jacobs. Not another soul knew about it—though Pattie, of course, has since learned the truth."

Before he let Favro go any further, Wallace wanted to know one thing: "Are you responsible for the deaths of Beckwith and Jacobs, or are they alive too?"

Even though it shouldn't have, the question took him by surprise. "No, no ... I'm sorry. The chief was natural causes, and Jacobs died while chasing Cyrus. He's a hero, sir. His wife should get the Medal of Honor on his behalf. I'm trusting it will all come out. The whole plan to track Cyrus was mine. All of it. And now that I've been arrested, it's got to stop. I can't go through a trial for something I didn't do. Especially as a detective working undercover."

Chief Wallace was trying his best to follow, but something was still confusing him. "Wait a second ... You did kill Dan Jacobs, didn't you?"

"Dan Jacobs had just fallen from the top of that building, breaking just about every bone in his body and crushing half his skull and all his organs. He begged me to shoot him through what was left of his heart, and I did it. If you want to say I killed him, I suppose I technically did, but it's a pretty twisted view. And then there's this ..."

Favro handed him the letter he'd received about Cyrus being his biological brother. Wallace read it slowly, and then set it down on the table. With a sigh, he pushed his thumb and index finger into the corner of his eyes, squinting hard and gritting his teeth. "Good Christian Anderson!" he said, raising his hand to his forehead.

"Oh, there's more," Favro said, and then went on to explain the whole mission and every single thing that had occurred over the past month.

"Once you compile all the evidence we've got, and everything your guys have put together, you should be able to find him. He's left a good footprint. My anger and ego have let this go on long enough. I do have one suggestion though, and I hope you'll seriously consider it."

"You wanna ask something of me? After all of this?"

"Yes, sir, I do. Are you familiar with Detective Sergeant Anthony Pucci from the Third District Headquarters?"

"Yes. He's their cold-case supervisor."

"Well, he knows me, sir. He's figured out who I am. Not only do I believe that he hasn't told a soul, but I think that he should have control of this case going forward. He's perfect for it."

"A cold-case supervisor?! From another district?"

"All the more reason. He's an outsider. Cyrus doesn't know him. Once he's been briefed on everything, just transfer him over for this case. It's not unusual. He's also used to working with the U.S. attorney. I'll bring him up to speed."

Chief Wallace sat very still with both palms flat on the table. It was clear he was considering something. He took his time in the process, then finally spoke. "I'm assuming your lawyer knows everything."

"Yes, sir."

"Well, if she's as smart as I hear she is, she'll agree with me. We can't break your cover right now. There will be so many charges brought against you and the force, it'll be the biggest scandal ever. They'll no doubt try to tie Beckwith and Jacobs's death to you somehow. God only knows what will happen to Pattie. We have to catch this guy before you come forward."

Favro was quick to agree. He only hoped the chief would take him up on his advice about Pucci.

Chief Wallace was firm on one thing. "You're finished as of right now. I wanna see you at Pattie's tomorrow after roll call, and I want all your physical evidence."

"How did you know I was staying at Pattie's?"

"Every officer in D.C. knows where you are, Phillip Caruso. You're a cop-killing bastard. Remember?"

Whoops! That wasn't good. He wasn't safe at all, and more importantly, neither was Pattie. Favro would have to consider relocating the two of them fast. This was the second warning he'd received. If anything happened to Pattie, he would never be able to live with himself.

The sun had set, and everything was now a dusky blue. Time for Cyrus to clock in. His work schedule started now. He had seen the news. Why was his new best friend leaving the courthouse with Pattie O'Rourke trailing behind? Pattie O'Rourke from Favro's precinct. Perhaps before torturing a police officer into telling him where Mr. Caruso was, he would pay a visit to Pattie's and snoop around.

It wasn't hard to find her address. But it wasn't quite dark enough for his Peeping Tom antics, so a cup of tea and the daily crossword would have to do for an hour or so. Cyrus sat at his usual spot at the counter in the truck stop down the road from his house. With his elbow on his knee and his hand over his mouth, he watched Edna in action.

"Oh, God, why didn't I kill that woman a long time ago," he mumbled to himself. It was almost too much for him to bear, but that kill would have been too close to home ... He couldn't chance it. Wouldn't want cops canvasing the area. His eyes darted from the crossword to the windows. The moment it was dark, he made his exit. It took him exactly twenty-eight minutes to reach Pattie's condo.

Just as he arrived there, Favro and Pattie arrived at the Palatial Tower All-Suite Hotel.

"Jack, are you kidding me?" She felt like they were on their honeymoon. This hotel was exquisite. You could not call it beautiful. Beautiful was not enough. It was fit for royalty. In fact, royalty *had* stayed there on more than one occasion.

"You deserve it," he said. "And after tonight, I don't feel comfortable bringing you home. We're staying here. We're going to stay here for a while. I like the privacy."

"What about Maxwell? My clothes? I need my personal things."

"I'm meeting the chief at your place tomorrow morning. Make a list. I'll get everything you need, or we'll buy it. Please tell me you have a cat carrier?"

She laughed out loud. "Yes, I do. It's in the front closet. But you have to get litter and cat food. Don't forget!"

"Ohh, listen to this," he said, spewing his sarcasm. "I gotta cater to that beast that doesn't even like me!"

"He'll love you soon enough, just like me." Pattie was smiling now. She was with her man, in a romantic place, and it seemed like she could finally take a safe breath. If she only knew what was really happening at that very moment back at home.

Cyrus sidled up to her patio doors and shone his flashlight inside. Her whole condo was dark. He listened carefully … Nothing. No alarm system.

"Pattie, Pattie, Pattie, what are you thinking? Someone could just walk right in and take whatever … they … want!" He popped the patio lock like it wasn't even there. Once inside, he drew the drapes and turned on a side lamp. That and his flashlight were all he needed. His hunt was forensic in nature. No one would ever know he'd been there, unless he wanted them to.

Cyrus moved from the living room to the kitchen. The two coffee cups in the sink were of particular interest. One with lip gloss and one without. He continued his search. The bedroom was next. He hesitated at the door. *Okay, that's unusual,* he thought. *Extremely feminine bedroom, broken bed. The bed did look antique, but why would she sleep on a broken bed?*

Just then, Maxwell passed through his legs and announced his entrance with a gentle meow. "Don't worry, pussy. Those days are long behind me."

Cyrus pointed his light toward the night table, and a piece of paper caught his eye. He padded over and picked it up.

Pattie,

Last night was incredible,
I have always loved you
and I will never leave you again!
Jack xoxo

Cyrus let the note drop free from his hand, and it fluttered through the air. He stood still in the dark, both arms dangling and the flashlight swaying. The absence of light hid the ghostly stare in his eyes. "Jack Favro … It was you who shot that cop. It was you. You're still alive."

CHAPTER 20

AS FAVRO UNLOCKED the door to their suite, Pattie squealed like a little girl. It was truly magnificent. The first thing to greet her were floor-to-ceiling windows and a view of the city that would knock anyone's socks off. She ran in, kicked off her boots, and dove onto the bed. Of course, she had to find it first. The place was three times the size of her condo.

"Excuse me, Your Highness, but wouldn't you like to look around a little?"

She turned and saw him standing in the opulent living area. A naughty thought came to mind. *He really is sexy, and I have a running start.* Favro smiled and knew immediately what she was thinking. He braced himself as she ran towards him and caught her midair. Their mouths opened in a gasp, and they locked quickly into a passionate kiss. The blue-velvet chaise lounge was their destination. She groaned as soon as her skin made contact with his.

Favro tried to slow the pace. He wanted this to last. But Pattie already had her blouse and camisole off and made short work of his clothes.

"Holy! What happened to my timid little office girl?"

"She's seen you naked!"

They stopped, looked into each other's eyes, and smiled. Then he kissed her on the neck gently, and she wrapped her arms around his enormous shoulders. He pulled the bow off her braid and carefully untwined it until her majestic locks flowed freely down her back. The most beautiful woman he had ever seen. His body took over, and he cradled her in his arms. Peeling her pants off with one hand was easy. Her petite frame hung onto him, and she wouldn't let go for anything in the world.

Favro laid her down on the chaise, and she moaned loudly. He kissed his way down her body to the sweet wet spot that could no longer be denied the pleasure it begged for. The room spun as she spiraled into an orgasm. Pushing her hips, his touch resonated deep within her.

Pattie could tell he wasn't finished with her yet. His erection was begging its way out of his jeans. She pulled at the button, and the zipper practically burst. She could barely lie still—he knew exactly what he was doing. Erotic thoughts flowed through her head. He was taking his time taking his clothes off. She bit down on her lip, hard.

That did it for him. It always had. Favro grabbed her by the hips, turning her over, then pulled her behind up against him so she could feel his erection. Pattie leaned forward and grasped the chaise while spreading her knees. Her legs were crossed at the ankles. She wanted him inside her, and she wanted him now. Her knees were braced on the velvet padding of the lounge as he slowly slid a finger inside her and kissed each shoulder blade.

As he buried his face in her flower-scented hair, she gave a sharp cry. "Oh… Jack!"

He slid into her then, and she pushed back, countering his thrusts move for move. Then he tipped his head back, finding his release. Groaning loudly and saying her name over and over, there was no denying how much he loved her. They collapsed, panting and holding each other. Neither wanted to move, but they eventually had to. The chaise was not big enough to hold them both comfortably. Their breathing slowed to a matching rhythm, and they were exhausted.

"Let's go to bed," he whispered.

"I love you so much, Jack."

"And I'm completely in love with you."

The next morning, Pattie opened her eyes and stretched out on a massive cloud. This bed was like none other she had seen or experienced. The billowy puffs of the silk duvet in the Presidential Suite engulfed her entire body. She reached for Favro, but he wasn't there. In his place was a yellow rose that matched those in the three massive vases of flowers in their room. And a note, signed, "Love Jack, XOXO."

He had gone to meet with the chief at her place, as planned. She was to relax and pamper herself, and they would be together again soon. One specific point was clear: Do not leave the room!

She could see that he had taken a shower. For her, a bubble bath and room service, in that order, would be perfect. Never had she experienced such decadence. The humongous jet tub was calling her name. She didn't know which bubble bath to choose, so she just closed her eyes and picked one. White Lotus it was, and twenty-five minutes in the tub wrinkled her up like a newborn baby. Pure ecstasy. The overwhelming feeling of great happiness didn't last long though as her thoughts wandered to Jack. *What is he going through right now? And is he okay?*

Favro waited patiently in Pattie's condo for the chief to arrive. He spent his time gathering all the proof he had on Cyrus Bircham from his evidence box and splayed it across the kitchen island. This included every single scrap of paper, photo likeness, and yellow sticky note he'd ever made. The 3D solid synthetic versions would have to wait a day. Parting with all of it was going to be hard, but he was starting to get comfortable with letting go of control.

Hot coffee and no booze. The shakes were coming less frequent now. At 9:10, there was a knock at the door. The chief had showed up as planned, and right behind him stood Pucci. Favro smiled.

The next two hours were thorough and grueling. However, they did agree on two things: Sharing all this evidence was certainly going to make finding Cyrus a whole lot easier, and it should have been done a long time ago. Chief Wallace was not exactly pleased with Favro, but his frustration would not serve them well at present as they tried to move forward. Pucci now had a large team at his disposal. Failure was no longer an option, and they would get right to work on Favro's leads.

Pucci had a second cup of tea before he left. He didn't drink coffee and had never had a cup in his life. The kettle was boiling, and so was Cyrus's blood as he hid behind the flowering dogwood bush under the living-room window. He had been there a long time. It was slightly ajar, and he had heard a lot. But nothing was as important as what he saw: Detective Jack Favro, sitting in Pattie's condo, only a knife's throw away. He only had one play left now. It would make Jack Favro suffer as much as possible, and he knew exactly how to do it.

Another twenty minutes passed before their meeting ended, and each went on their way. Favro had no idea how gruesome things were about to become. He was being followed, and he was about to bring this ferocious serial killer right to Pattie.

Janine's meeting with Karen Davis went remarkably well. One couldn't say she was satisfied with the information Janine provided, but she wasn't angry either. It wasn't the first undercover case she'd dealt with. It was not being informed for so long that brought her displeasure. She had people to answer to, and she'd have to make a case for not charging Favro with a crime of any kind, nor Pattie with aiding and abetting. One thing everyone seemed to agree on though: Nobody would out Favro until they'd apprehended Cyrus Bircham.

Favro's cell rang. It was Janine. He would always take her call no matter what.

"Well, my friend," she said, "it seems you're off the hook for now. I managed to placate the U.S. attorney with the promise of new updates on a daily basis."

"I'll forward you everything I have as I know it, and I'll make sure Chief Wallace does the same. He's not happy, though."

Janine was not surprised. "I'm not used to dealing with happy, so we'll get along just fine. Don't worry about that."

He took a deep breath. "If I haven't said it yet, or enough, thank you for everything you've done for me."

She hesitated a moment. "You've said it, and you're welcome, Jack. We're not near finished, but I know you've been through hell. I'd say let's have a drink when this is over, but how about I just have one for each of us now?"

He could tell she was smiling, and it made him feel like she was confident, so he smiled too.

"That sounds like a great idea. I'll hold you to it."

As Favro pulled up to the hotel, he shut the car off and sat a while. He was worn out, but some good food, sleep, and Pattie were all he wanted. He couldn't wait to see her. He wanted to lie in bed and feel her fall asleep in his arms. Intertwined like the roots of a tree, never coming apart. He surprised himself, feeling no desire to reach under the seat for a drink. Things were changing. Things were promising.

Six spots over, in a black SUV hybrid, sat Cyrus Bircham. The tinted windows gave him good cover. He watched Favro make his way from Pattie's 29 Serval EV to the entrance of the hotel. He looked completely at ease.

"Thought you were smarter than me, I suppose, Mr. Man?" Cyrus hissed. "Slaughtering your girlfriend will be my finest hour!"

He had all the patience in the world for this final act. It would be his best work.

Favro gave the secret knock and unlocked the door to their suite, not wanting to scare Pattie by sneaking in. She had been busy putting the personal valet to work. Stretched out on the blue-velvet chaise, Pattie was exquisite in a coral-silk negligee with cream-lace trim. Her long hair was down, and he instantly forgot he was hungry. Just standing there staring at her made everything right in the world. She smiled, and he started toward her.

"Oh, no, no … Tonight is all about you, my love." Pattie met him halfway and took his hand in hers, leading him to the luxurious bathroom where bubbles and scented candles awaited. "You, my darling, are going to take a bubble bath, and I am going to wash your back," she said, doing her best impression of Marilyn Monroe in the Presidential Suite.

Pattie tenderly removed every single piece of Favro's clothing and led him into the sensuous bath. The water intimately cradled his body, and he could feel his muscles relaxing. The tension in his neck slipped away as she gently held his head in her hands. Then she poured cups of warm water over his scalp, massaged gently, and almost put him to sleep. Finally, she patiently bathed him from head to toe, and when she was finished, she used the same care to dry him off with an enormous Egyptian towel.

The double XL hotel robe and slippers looked fantastic on him! And Martin, their valet, had just about everything on the lunch menu waiting for them in the dining room, each dish covered with a silver dome, including dessert.

They lounged and ate and talked and ate until even the idea of making love could not come before sleep. All the blinds were pulled, and the darkness made it feel like midnight instead of midday. They crawled up onto their cloud, kissed and kissed, and then fell asleep holding hands.

Would this delightful occurrence take place at the ending of a lovely fairytale? Or would it be the beginning of a horror story where night terrors became real, and they never fell asleep together again?

CHAPTER 21

CYRUS HAD WAITED exactly two minutes from the time Favro entered the hotel, passed the front desk, and walked into the elevator before he made his own suave entrance and approached the concierge. A professional looking woman in her early thirties greeted him.

"Good afternoon, sir. May I be of assistance today?"

Cyrus used his sexy voice. "Yes, you most certainly can. The gentleman who was just in here, I'd like to do something for him and his new bride."

Her demeanor changed as she stared at him. A spell had been cast.

"It's quite alright… I know he's paid a lot for his privacy. You see, I was his best man, and I'd like to pay for their room service for the length of their stay. It's a gift, so I don't want them to know about it until they leave. Can we work that out somehow?"

Immediately, this professional woman became very impressionable, and he knew that he had convinced her. She looked down at her computer screen, and then back up at him.

"They've already charged a fair amount. Would you like to pay for that as well?" She was smiling ear to ear and so was Cyrus, pleased with his triumph.

"Of course! Absolutely everything, including valet service and gratuities. But it must remain a complete secret. I insist on that. It wouldn't be a surprise otherwise."

She was swayed by this striking man and his kindness and was about to become extremely loyal as well. Cyrus slid five crisp hundred bills across the desk to her. "Oh, no, sir, I couldn't possibly—"

"Your services are never rewarded well enough, I'm sure." He gave her his famous grin that secretly said that she'd now do whatever he said … and he was right. She was giving him the room number, the floor, the name on the receipt (Caruso) … everything. He, of course, gave her a false name, identification, and credit card number, all of which went through just fine.

He winked at her. "I'll look forward to seeing you again."

She couldn't scribble down her work schedule fast enough. What was it about him?

Cyrus made a fair guess that Favro and Pattie wouldn't be going anywhere that night, so it was safe to head back to his home and prepare. It had been a while since he'd sent a letter to Favro, but he shouldn't take a chance and scare him off. Still … his sick mind couldn't hold him back completely. He would write a little note … a little note to the chief to be received once it was too late for him to do anything.

When he arrived back at his house, Cyrus had that familiar feeling he often got before going to work. The one that interfered with his sleep. There would not be much sleep in his house tonight. He would have to spend his day tomorrow outside the hotel, hoping Favro would leave Pattie alone long enough for him to make an entrance.

Cyrus stood in front of his desk and thought for a moment. *Should I handwrite or use the computer?* After a moment, he'd decided: *Handwriting it is.* He wanted to make his last letter special. This one was far more intimate to him, so it called for a more intimate hand. He reached for a sheet of blank paper and wrote:

DEAR CHIEF WALLACE,

THIS ONE YOU KNOW,

WITH SKIN SO FAIR.

BEFORE I SLAUGHTER,

I'LL CUT OFF HER HAIR!!

Just a little note this time. No need to brag. His work would say it all. By the time the chief got this, his job would be done. Cyrus laughed out loud, then brought his hand quickly to his mouth. Grinning beneath his palm and looking from side to side, he remembered that there was no need to contain his glee, so he burst into laughter again. No, he would not sleep much tonight. Hot chocolate and "The Pit and the Pendulum" would help him pass the evening.

"Nothing like a nice short horror story before bed."

He took the note he'd written, slipped it into an envelope, and addressed it to Chief Wallace. Then he set out to the kitchen to put his shiny copper kettle on to boil. Tomorrow would be a big day.

Favro was the first to open his eyes. It was not unusual for him to wake up early now. However, seeing such beauty lying next to him was definitely something he wanted to get used to. Sleeping soundly, Pattie looked like the front cover of a romance novel. He slipped out from between the sheets, and she didn't even stir. Next to the bed, he saw the clothes Pattie had laid out for him the day before.

He headed for the bathroom to shave and dress. His hair was starting to grow back, forming a dark shadow on his scalp in place of the one formerly on his chin. He thought he cleaned up nicely. And for her, he wanted to. The clothes fit him perfectly. And a new leather jacket! Life was good again. The only thing he wanted to hear now was that Cyrus Bircham was in custody. But that wasn't up to him anymore.

He grabbed another yellow rose from the vase by the door and laid it by Pattie's head. He scribbled a note for her to order breakfast and told her he'd be back by nine-thirty. Then Favro was out the door to run an overdue errand. The initial plan had been that once he and Pattie checked into the hotel room, they would not leave again until Cyrus was caught. But something troubled Favro greatly, and he just couldn't let it go another day.

Two of his close comrades had died, and he'd never gotten a chance to properly salute them. With everything they had done for him, everything they'd given up for him, he'd never gotten to say goodbye. He was going to visit their graves. The sun was shining. He felt calm and relaxed. Today was a day to make amends.

He left the hotel feeling like he was going to do a good thing. And so did Cyrus, who had his eyes locked on Favro from his spot in the parking lot some twenty yards away. He had been sitting in his SUV since five o'clock that morning. The corner of his mouth curled up.

"Take your time, my friend. Take your time." Cyrus waited exactly ten minutes after Favro pulled out of the lot before making a move. Just in case something had been forgotten, always wait ten minutes. That was the home-invasion rule. Time was up. Time to play. He picked up the huge gift basket of chocolate, fruit, and wine from the seat next to him and proceeded to the hotel entrance. It was a busy morning. People passed him, coming and going. He was barely noticed, until he reached the elevator, where a valet stepped in front of him.

"May I help you with that, sir?" the man asked, mistaking him for a guest.

Cyrus put his determined head down and proceeded. "No, thank you."

The valet was unwavering. "I'm more than happy to carry that for you, sir."

"I'm more than happy to slice your throat for you," Cyrus imagined saying but didn't. The elevator doors closed with just the two of them inside. "This is a personal delivery I'm making, and I'm fine, thank you."

Cyrus had a specific ability to deal with people easily and without friction, but this guy didn't know when to quit. "Special deliveries are supposed to be left at the front desk," the man said then, somewhat curtly. "You should know that … *delivery man!"*

Cyrus lowered the basket from his face and moved toward the valet, hissing through his teeth. "Do I look like one of your fuckin' delivery boys, asshole?"

The once confident valet tucked his chin in tight and smashed himself up against the elevator wall. "No, sir! I'll just be getting off at the next floor."

And he did, running off the elevator as the doors closed behind him. Cyrus was relieved. He never veered from his plans, and he would have killed that bastard valet if he hadn't let up. That would have been a shame. He was extremely disciplined and hated wavering from his intent. When the doors opened on the tenth floor, Cyrus proceeded to his destination like he had walked the hallways a hundred times. Always confident, always systematic. When he reached the door, he smiled, tilted his head back, and inhaled deeply. Victory awaited him.

Tapping on the door five times, he declared, "Room service, ma'am!"

Pattie was scrolling through the news on the chaise lounge and immediately became alarmed. "I didn't order any room service. Take it away!" She was quite stern about it. Jack's rules were very strict.

"It's from Mr. Caruso, ma'am. He said to make sure you received it."

And just like that, her guard was down. She raced to the door, with her coral kimono covering her negligee, and didn't even look through the peep hole. She just opened the door to the huge gift basket covering Cyrus's face.

Pattie was so excited. "Oh, my goodness! Come right in!" she exclaimed.

And of course, Cyrus did exactly as requested.

"Just set it on the marble table, please."

He was most accommodating, despite hiding a roll of duct tape on his left wrist, some yellow braid rope, and a knife so scary that one might have a heart attack upon seeing before someone even had an opportunity to use it.

Pattie couldn't take her eyes off the basket as she poked and prodded through the decadent delights. And Cyrus couldn't take his eyes off of her. He lingered a little beside her with his hands behind his back.

"Oh, I'm so sorry," she said suddenly, realizing her rudeness. "You'll be very generously taken care of when my husband and I leave the hotel. Please just leave your name at the front desk before you go … and thank you again."

Cyrus pulled the duct tape from his wrist, then the yellow rope and the knife he'd hidden beneath his clothes. He was parched for a good slow torture, and Pattie would definitely quench his thirst. When she turned to face him, the light from the chandelier bounced off the knife's blade. There was nowhere to run … but she sure tried.

Favro had just arrived at Jacobs's grave site. He knew exactly what he wanted to say, having thought about it in the car ride over. His ego must have been waning because he'd finally realized that it wasn't about everything this rookie had done for him at all. It was about the obstacles and fears he had overcome for himself. Favro was so bloody proud of him that he actually started to tear up. And that's when it happened …

The alarm on his cell phone went off. At the quiet grave site, the sound was piercing. For a brief moment, he was taken aback. Then it hit him. The panic button! The alarm he'd set up on Pattie's phone! She'd hit it!

Favro bolted as fast as he could for the car, even as he tried to call her, which was a near impossibility with the horrible shaking of his panicked hands. The only other thing he could think to do was drive as fast as he could.

What would make her hit that button? What was happening to her right now? His face grimaced in every possible way. He flew through stop signs and yellow lights like they weren't even there, at one point missing a busload of people by mere inches. The seventeen-minute drive was sheer agony, so he made it in twelve. When he arrived at the suite, he was too late.

It was all over.

CHAPTER 22

PATTIE HAD NO idea that the man standing in front of her was Cyrus Bircham. She had never seen his picture. But the fact remained that he was there. She was not dreaming. He had a monstrous knife, and he was positioned between her and the door. Game on!

Pattie's body took flight. She grabbed her cell phone, hitting the panic button as she soared over the chaise lounge. As fast as she ran though, he was only one second behind her, stretching and grabbing for her around every piece of furniture and every turn and corner. That's when she made the biggest error of her life. She ran into the huge bathroom, which had only one exit that he quickly moved to block. She hurled every single item she could grab in his direction, but he came at her relentlessly.

With one last grab for her ankle, he had her. As she tripped, they both fell into the sunken tub, which was more like a small pool than something to bathe in. He didn't want to kill her there. Cyrus had another plan. Grabbing for her throat, he was on top of her back. Pattie was kicking with everything she had, scrambling to get free of him and out of the tub, her arms flailing everywhere. Then her right elbow hit his temple like it had a target on it.

The blow knocked Cyrus back far enough for Pattie to get her footing. Out of the tub she flew. In less than two seconds, he was back on his feet and back on her trail. Man, that girl could run! With bare feet and coral kimono flying behind her, she looked like a superhero.

She would *have* to be one to get away from him. As they ran through the suite, he caught up with her by the dining-room table and grabbed hold of her long braid. The sharp yank stopped her in her tracks. She twirled around to face him, and his right fist connected with her left cheekbone—hard—and knocked her clean out.

Cyrus worked quickly then. Dragging her across the marble floor, the thrill of the looming kill made his cheeks flush. This never happened. She was special. He tied Pattie to the gold tapestry chair in the sitting room. He wasn't so attractive anymore, not with the twisted look of glee on his face.

Hands and feet secured and a rope around her neck, Pattie wasn't going anywhere. But Cyrus always kept his word, remembering his note: *Before I slaughter, I'll cut off her hair.* So, that was his first order of business.

As Pattie was coming to, he grabbed hold of her long braid, and with one quick slice of his sharp knife, she had a new hairstyle. She was fully conscious now and realized what he had done. Before Pattie could object, debate, or scream, a piece of duct tape flew over her mouth.

Cyrus wanted to leave lots of hugs and kisses for Favro before he slit her throat. So he started with her arms, and then made his way down her legs, carving small *X*'s and *O*'s along the way, while she wept and tried hard to scream past the tape on her mouth.

Her negligee was soaking up the blood as he carved the word FOREVER into the back of her neck. Cyrus was pleased with himself. It was time to finish her off. He raised the blade to Pattie's throat, closed his eyes, and took a deep breath …

Then the door to the suite flung open. Cyrus whipped his head around to find himself staring at Anthony Pucci. One bullet flew from the man's gun, grazing Cyrus's left thigh. Although it had only caught the meat of his leg, it was enough to make him drop the knife and fall to the floor. Pucci raced to kick the blade out of the way, just as Cyrus grabbed for it. They both slipped on the glossy floor, smeared with both Pattie's and Cyrus's blood. Pucci's gun slid one way and the knife slid the other.

This could easily have come down to a punching match, but Pucci made sure this would never happen. There would be no match at all. Cyrus was injured, and Pucci kept waylaying until Cyrus no longer moved. Then he cuffed him to the marble table and went to check on Pattie. He pulled the tape off her mouth and cradled her gently.

"Hang in there, sweetie." he said. A few moments later he called for an ambulance and a shitload of cops. "You're gonna be okay."

He untied her hands and feet, and the rope around her neck. She was bleeding badly. Whipping the damask cloth off the dining table, he wrapped her up and held her tight.

Just hang on, he thought. *Just hang on.* She was passing out in his arms.

Then came Favro, skidding through the doorway with a look of horror on his face. He was too late. He had missed it all. Seeing Pattie in the state she was in, and Cyrus cuffed to the table with a psychotic grin on his face, was just too much to bear. He had finally reached his breaking point.

Pouncing viciously on Cyrus, Favro didn't care that it wasn't a fair fight and started pounding on him. Still cuffed to the table, Cyrus was now the one bleeding profusely, and unless someone stepped in, Favro would kill him. Pucci considered this for one second and thought perhaps he would just let it happen. Then he thought better of it and laid Pattie down so that he could tear Favro off of Cyrus's limp form.

"Stop! Buddy, stop! He's done!" Pucci assured him.

Favro was sweating profusely and breathing like he had run a marathon. He could hardly believe what had taken place in his absence and lay on the floor in a bewildered daze.

"How in the hell did this happen?"

"I got the alert on my phone, just like you," Pucci responded. "Thank God I was close."

Pattie moaned, and Favro was instantly alert. He leapt to her side. Her pale body made him shudder. She managed to blink up at him, and his rage for Cyrus made his stomach turn. He wished he had killed him. Less than a minute later, the suite was full of police officers and EMTs. Pattie was taken care of, and Cyrus was taken down.

"You go with her," Pucci said. "I'll go with him."

"Am I in trouble?" Favro asked.

"Nope." Pucci smiled. "Janine's got your back."

Favro smiled at him. "Thanks, partner. Please don't take your eyes off him."

"Not for one second, buddy. Not for one bloody second. I can promise you that."

Pattie was taken directly to the Howard University Hospital. She had lost a fair amount of blood, and some of her wounds were quite deep. Her hospital stay would be lengthy. Cyrus was tended to by an EMT, then hogtied and taken into custody. He would need medical attention, but they weren't too concerned about his pain or discomfort at present. It would be solitary confinement for him from here on out.

The mayor had finally gotten his wish. And the headline in the morning edition of *The D.C. Liberty* said it all: "SERIAL KILLER CAPTURED."

Favro was exhausted. The psychological toll the killings had taken on him was substantial. What Cyrus had done to Pattie, the woman he loved ... That was something his heart could barely take, and the guilt was overwhelming. The only thing that would bring him peace now would be seeing Cyrus in the Tank, serving ten years for every murder he'd committed.

If the U.S. attorney got her way, Dan Jacobs's death would be included in that toll. That would make it seventy consecutive years. Favro imagined Cyrus sliding into that water and the buttons not working. Oh, how that would make his dreams come true!

It was two months before Cyrus came to trial, with him getting quite comfortable in his solitary confinement. Even though he'd pulled the most lenient judge in D.C. and had a strong defense with an insanity plea, nothing was going to save him now. The charges against him were so lengthy that it took almost ten minutes to read them all in court. The trial lasted sixteen days, and the jury was out for only twenty-one minutes.

Cyrus Bircham was found guilty on all counts but one. They could not prove him responsible for Dan Jacobs's death beyond a reasonable doubt, which would be a hard resentment for Favro to get over.

The day arrived, and the chaplain was making his way down to talk to Cyrus. He wondered whether a miracle would happen and he would show some remorse. That would make this encounter so much easier. But God never hinted that things would be easy, only that he'd have a full-time job that would last a lifetime.

Death row was pretty much exactly as one might imagine. People didn't stay there very long now. You were an animal, waiting your turn to free up your cage. No posters or pictures on the walls, and the cells were very tiny. No luxury items whatsoever. No bars for a door, just concrete with a small slot for food to be passed through, or for your hands to be held out of and cuffed.

When the chaplain reached the wing, he asked the guard, "What did he have for his last meal?"

The guard shook his head. "Didn't ask for one and didn't finish the one we gave him."

The chaplain's eyebrows raised. "Really?"

"Yup. Goin' to sleep with no supper, I guess."

The chaplain didn't find that very amusing, but he did find it interesting. Was it possible the serial killer was depressed? Or perhaps he had made his own kind of peace … The guard pulled a chair up for him outside the cell, then left the two men alone.

Cyrus spoke calmly but with intent from his place behind the wall. "I can hear you breathing out there, Padre, but they won't let me see you. Was that your choice?"

"Not at all, my son. I would gladly see you," the chaplain answered calmly.

"You call me your son. I've never been anybody's son, really."

"God is your Father, and you are his son."

"Well, then I don't think my father was much of a mentor to me … for me to end up in this predicament. Wouldn't you agree, Padre?"

The chaplain smiled slightly, enjoying the little jab. "Did you ever ask him for help? Because God's just been waiting there, every day, for you to ask."

Cyrus hissed at him. "I don't know any son that should have to *ask* his father for help!"

The chaplain remained composed. "Every relationship is about love, Cyrus. About being open to love. Accepting love, giving love, wanting love, asking for love … The more you give, the more you get. You love yourself; you love others. And when you struggle, you ask for help."

"Oh, Padre, you're quite naive, aren't you? Don't you think a baby needs to *receive* love in order to learn how to give it?" Cyrus was quite pleased with this challenge he'd presented to the chaplain.

"My son, if you do not receive love, you must give it to *yourself*. And if you have trouble doing that, you must ask your Father. He will always oblige."

Cyrus laughed out loud, thanked the chaplain for his time, then said simply, "Go back where you came from. You've got no business here. No confessions from me, Padre, and you've got no last rights to perform. No bread and wine and sprinkling of holy water on my head. I loved all right. I loved everything I did, and all of my night terrors will be fairytales compared to what I've already lived through. Don't waste your time praying for me. I'll be just fine."

Cyrus didn't speak again. The chaplain squeezed his lips into a thin line and shook his head. It was time for him to go. There was nothing more for him to say.

Thirty minutes later, twenty-four people gathered to watch Cyrus Bircham carry out his sentence. Some relatives of the victims, the media, Chief Wallace, and Jack Favro all sat behind the curtains in the room adjacent to the Narcoleptic Sleep Tank. At exactly eleven a.m., the drapes would open, and they would all witness trauma and peace at the same time. Either way, it would finally be over.

They all sank down in their seats, roosting uncomfortably and murmuring quietly to each other, waiting for the hour to strike. Favro didn't move or say a thing. This made Chief Wallace more nervous than he already was. He knew Jack pretty well now, but he had no idea what his reaction would be to what was about to take place. He didn't know what his own reaction would be. Taking a peek at Favro, he just wanted it to be over.

No camera equipment was allowed in the viewing area. Pen and paper. That was it. Then it was eleven a.m., and a little red light flashed on the wall beside the draped window, and the curtains split in two, opening wide and revealing the monstrous tank of water. It was truly terrifying, especially if one's imagination was running full throttle. The guard in the viewing room reminded everybody to remain in their seats until the "execution of the sentence had ruled."

What the hell does that mean! Favro thought. *Until he's dead? Until he's asleep? What?!*

He was getting antsy now, fidgeting in his seat and regretting his choice to sit in the front row. No changing seats now. *Game on …*

The chute at the top of the tank opened then, and a naked Cyrus Bircham slid headfirst into the water that would seal his fate. Quickly getting his bearings, he swam forward and hit the glass hard, sticking to it like a frog with his hands and feet. Everyone in the viewing room pulled their heads back a few inches in unison, as though they'd all just been rear-ended by the same car. The shock factor of his movement had been huge, but there was still more to come.

Cyrus stuck out his tongue then, displaying a shiny silver razor blade. Then he reached for it with his long fingers and proceeded to slice his left arm wide open from wrist to elbow in one fast motion. The water in the tank was no longer calm, or clear, and neither was the viewing room. Total mayhem had ensued. As the water turned red, chairs toppled over and people pushed their way backwards, screaming wildly to be let out of the room.

Everyone except Favro, who did not move an inch at first as he struggled to see Cyrus through the increasingly bloody water. Then slamming his hands up against the glass window, he squinted as hard as he could. Moving his head from left to right, he couldn't find him, and then all of a sudden, the room that held the Narcoleptic Sleep Tank went black, and the curtains closed.

"No!" Favro screamed. "NOOOO!!!"

The chief made his way over to him and grabbed the back of his jacket with all his strength, almost tearing it from his body as he fought to pull him away from the window. He was no match for Favro's muscles though, and the crowd of viewers was now becoming hostile. One guard was trying to calm everybody and radio for help at the same time. It was futile. They pushed right past her and tumbled out into the hallway. As far as they were concerned, it was over … but not for Favro. Never for Favro.

He hadn't gotten to see him die.

CHAPTER 23

TIME PASSED BY, and the women of Washington D.C. were finally resting easier. Favro had been assured over and over that Cyrus would never be a threat to anybody ever again. It was finally finished, for good. He was gone.

He retired from the force and became quite comfortable living with Pattie in her condo. They were a couple. He had decided that he would start doing a little P.I. work on the side. But not for a while. A little downtime together was in order, and maybe even a vacation. Lord knows they both could use it. However, a romantic evening between two lovers was just not meant to be. Not tonight. Pattie and Jack had just settled into their cozy sofa to relax. And that's when it happened…

They were nearly deafened by the sound of the patio doors shattering in an explosion of glass right in front of their eyes. Out of the destruction emerged Cyrus Bircham. He was alive. With a grotesque pink scar from wrist to elbow, he was alive and standing in their living room with one thing on his mind: murder.

Favro was up in an instant, and they were on each other, rolling across the floor. Cyrus kicked him hard in the head, and they broke apart. Pattie was curled up in the smallest ball possible behind her tea cart in the corner of her living room. Her antique cups adorned its top shelf, and she was pitching them like grenades with all of her might at Cyrus. Finally finding her brave heart, she thrust herself forward with the teapot and smashed it over the back of Cyrus's head.

He turned to her with a quizzical look, then grabbed her throat, lifting her clear off the ground. She grabbed for his hands, struggling to free herself as her legs kicked wildly in the air. Then Favro came to her rescue. With one fierce punch to the killer's kidneys, he dropped her to a painful crumple on the floor. She scampered quickly back behind her tea-cart bunker.

Cyrus's mission was clear. It was time for Favro to die. He rose to his feet with a purpose, and reaching behind him, he pulled two push daggers from the back of his pants. Splaying his arms out into the air, he was ready to attack. Favro swung around to meet him. Stretching high for his wrists, he grabbed on tight and kneed Cyrus in the stomach. Cyrus dropped one of the daggers, and Favro kicked it under the sofa. The other dagger was still firmly in Cyrus's palm though, with the blade jutting out through his fingers, as he slowly bent Favro's wrist backwards, trying to puncture his neck.

Their arms were shaking in their effort to resist each other's holds. Favro hit Cyrus hard between the eyes with his forehead, and the two of them broke their hold and scrambled to gain composure. Cyrus made some swiping motions with his fists, though they were no match for Favro's. The push dagger in his hand could quickly end this fight. It was designed to puncture, and Cyrus knew every potential kill shot.

Time to even things up, Favro thought as he grabbed his Glock from its holster on the kitchen island, but a round-house kick from Cyrus sent it flying through the air. Ohhh ... *That* pissed him off.

"You wanna play?" Favro yelled. "Let's go!" He took a deliberate step toward his lethal opponent, grabbing the arm with the dagger and twisting it hard, hyperextending the elbow and drawing a yelp from Cyrus's throat. Favro had him in an armbar now and proceeded to punch him four times in the ribs before pushing him backwards to the ground. Still, Cyrus would not stay down, crawling over the ottoman with blood dripping from the side of his mouth and a cut over his eye. Favro turned away, and Cyrus attempted to reach for his leg.

Bad decision. He was instantly met with a roundhouse kick similar to the one he himself had thrown only moments earlier. Apparently they'd *both* had martial-arts training. The push dagger finally fell from Cyrus's grip, and they both made a grab for it. Cyrus got there first and plunged it into Favro's thigh.

With all Favro's meat and muscle, this hurt like hell but was not enough to take him down. He pulled it right back out and lunged forward, shoving it straight into Cyrus's jugular.

A look of horror appeared on the serial killer's face then, one that it had never worn before. His long fingers clenched around the blade, and he pulled it out, the emerging tip releasing a high arc of blood that left splatter marks on the ceiling, and then everywhere else. The blood from the wound just kept pumping and pumping, even as Cyrus scrambled at his neck to make it stop.

He could not.

Collapsing against the sofa, beaten and bruised, his arms fell limp, and then just hung heavily at his sides, even as his chin dropped down upon his chest, which had risen and fallen for the final time at last.

Favro leaned in close and whispered to Cyrus, "It may be a little late, but I've been waiting a long time to say this to you:

I'm the Murder Police, and you're under arrest, you son of a bitch!"

Suddenly, Cyrus lunged forward, with the push dagger from under the sofa, and jammed it into Favro's chest. Out it came and in it went, over and over, puncturing his lungs until he couldn't breathe. He could only listen helplessly as Pattie started screaming his name and grabbing for him. Then he jerked up in bed, sweating profusely and struggling for air as his heart beat out of his chest. It had been over a year since he'd closed the Cyrus case.

"For the love of God, how long will these night terrors last?!"

The End

EPILOGUE

Yes, it had been over a year since he'd closed the Cyrus case and watched him bleed out in that horrible tank of slowly reddening water. His biological brother had opted out of his sentence—with the same gruesome flair that Favro had witnessed from him far too often at his crime scenes—unwilling to face the punishing promise of perpetual terror. And in his passing, he'd left Favro with one final scene of horror to remember him by. To haunt him.

Favro had his own debt to pay. How much sooner might Cyrus have been caught if not for his own stubbornness? If not for placing his own pride in the pursuit over the well-being of the public? Over the lives of those women he'd never met … and even over the one woman he loved more than anything else.

His brother escaped his punishment, taking the coward's way out … but Favro paid for years to come. He didn't have to spend time in the tank to experience night terrors. His PTSD served them up regularly. But Pattie helped him every day by convincing him that peace is not a solo journey.

A Psychiatrist's Note on Night Terrors:

Extremely distressing and disturbing night terrors can have a profound negative effect on more than just an individual's sleep. They also affect mental health, physical health, and quality of life.

These repeated awakenings from major sleep with detailed recall of extended and extremely frightening dreams are associated with post-traumatic stress disorder.

Trauma-related nightmares occur during the deepest stage of non-rapid-eye-movement (NREM) sleep.

Dr. Muni Mysore MBBS, FRCP©
Winnipeg, Manitoba, Canada

A Word from the Author

The opinions expressed here, regarding any form of mental illness, are mine and mine alone. I state them freely. They are what have occurred during my life, therapy, and experiences with the many people I have been fortunate enough to know and befriend over the course of what I'll call "my journey."

I want to add these comments about my night terrors so that people might better understand them. Sometimes, they play out with full dialogue. Sometimes, there are thought processes that come fully formed with a complete understanding of what is playing out, and I can even foresee what is to come, terrified of the outcome but unable to change it, even though I've had that same night terror over and over.

Other times, horrific scenes play out with more and more detail added over time. Lasting weeks, months, and even years. And lastly, like a train running off the tracks, I can do nothing to stop it, and I am most certainly always among the casualties.

Horrific, terrifying, and when untreated ... a threat of insanity that has been biting at my heels for most of my life.

Depression and anxiety are two subjects that are now openly discussed in our society. As a result, not only are the highest ever number and quality of recovery options available, but more people are asking for help daily. But the stigma that long surrounded these issues delayed the development of successful treatment and recovery options for many years.

It is my wish that we now try speaking more openly, and to a greater degree, about PTSD by doing so openly with our friends, our families, our employers, and the public at large.

People are suffering, and the "don't talk, don't tell, don't speak, don't feel" approach is the enemy, derailing any chance of improving our quality of life. We are not weak if we speak unashamedly about that with which we struggle.

If you did not cause something, and are unable to control it, you are not to blame for it.

If you were a child of abuse, you are not to blame. If you saw suffering, you are not to blame. If you were forced to do something against your will, you are not to blame. If you were or are in the military, you cannot blame yourself for uncontrollable occurrences **or** the outcome/consequences of orders you have carried out.

Of course, people ask, "If I have no control, how do I get well?"

I have found, from personal experience, that acceptance is the first key. Accepting ourselves for who we are is true love and a kindness we give to ourselves. The weakness comes from *not* loving yourself. We cannot change the past. We can only choose our journey forward.

For people who have uncontrolled depression, anxiety, post-traumatic stress disorder, or other mental-health issues, self-love does not come easy. In fact, we do not quite understand it.

It is a learned behavior and requires a lot of work, and sometimes medication as well. That part is for a physician to decide. Do not be ashamed. No one is better than you. We are all imperfect human beings. We are all different from each other in unique ways.

Our trials may seem never-ending. We may feel exhausted. Be gentle with yourself. Go slowly. The best things happen slowly. You do not have to be "better" by any certain time. And please don't compare yourself to others. You cannot have success without failure.

If you focused on how many people actually judge you, you would be surprised to learn how many people don't. Everyone—every color, size, ability or disability, rich or poor—has their own set of complicated problems. It is all relative.

I have dealt with many things and continue to do so on my journey: PTSD, clinical depression, anxiety, epilepsy, and fibromyalgia, just to name a few. I might have a lot on my plate, but I also have many tools to cope with it. And I give myself permission to use every one of them, every day.

However, one problem that has haunted me from childhood, and followed me to adulthood, is night terrors. When I was a little girl, they were just "bad dreams." When I was a teenager, they were "nightmares." But it wasn't until I became an adult that I learned the true meaning of the horrors I'd struggled with all those years.

Night terrors, or sleep terrors, can last about ten minutes, but they have been known to last as long as thirty to forty minutes during the deepest stage of NREM sleep. When you think of how fast you dream, even ten minutes can be a long time to be terrorized. And for most of my life, I had no tools to help me cope.

You can work diligently with many accredited sources during your waking hours (and you should) to deal with your PTSD. Night terrors, if you suffer from them, can be hard to control, but they are part and parcel of the disorder. Having said that, it is possible to treat them. It was when I started being treated for PTSD that things got better.

I am at a point in my life now where I have very few night terrors. Some still make me cry out, and some are just violent in nature. But I recover faster. Is that because of acceptance? Because of an exceptional psychiatrist and medication? Because of all the hard work I've put into my recovery? Or do I finally just care about and love myself enough not to give up?

Get treatment for your PTSD. You're worth it.

As I write this, I'm smiling. I know that when I struggle, when sounds are too loud, and lights are too bright, and crowds are too big, and I feel like I'm failing, I remember one thing: I'm at the bottom of the circle, and there's nowhere to go but up. I *will* have joy again. That's how life's circle works. I try not to stay at the bottom too long. There are beautiful things to see at the top. So, I will talk, and I will feel, and I will speak, and I will tell … until somebody listens.

Maybe it will be you.

Good luck … and have a peaceful night's sleep.

Donna Galloway

Special Thanks To:

John Galloway

Kelly McDougall

Sandra & Peter Mignacca

Dr. Muni Mysore

Solmaz Nafez

Doris Klassen

Dennis & Joan Walker

Mike Altham

Dr. Frank Renouf

Dr. Johann Raubenheimer

Kelly Bond

Wajih Zeid

Malcom Bell

Dr. Christopher Bourque

Wes Schilke

Calvin Schilke

Rosa Giampaolo

Gordon Stanger

Terry & Donny White

Extended family & friends

My Readers

To my husband, Johnny: For allowing me into your incredible world of anonymity. To watch you give so selflessly to others. For your tolerance and patience. For all the sleep you lost when I woke up screaming. For better or worse, in sickness and in health, you've certainly picked me up off the floor more times than you ever should have had to. For working so hard while I couldn't and supporting me through the process. For all the laughter in our marriage and for always holding my hand. You are the strongest man I know, and I am a better woman today because of you. For all of this, I thank you. I wish all of God's Blessings on you always, I love you.

To Kelly McDougall: What is a writer without their editor? If you say successful, you are lying. When I met Kelly for the first time, she was full of enthusiasm and positivity. A shining light. I knew right away that she understood me. Kelly is extremely talented and a brilliant writer. I count myself very fortunate and grateful that she agreed to edit my book. I often pondered this as I wrote: *"She'll read this and wonder if the same person she met wrote it."* However, her feedback made me a better writer. As a result, I became more excited about the process. For all of this and for you, I thank you.

To Sandra Mignacca: Sandra is my "faithful" friend. It's a personal thing, and she'll know what I mean by that. Our chats inspire me; they give me hope and bring me an incredible sense of calm. That is her personality. She is a gentle soul. Everyone who knows her loves her. She has the most admirable moral values and sets an example every single day. She has changed my life for the better, and often reminds me of what's really important: "You're not in charge." This is a lesson that's proven so valuable. For all of this, and your friendship, I thank you.

To Peter Mignacca: They say it is wonderful to know someone who knows a little about a lot. In Peter, I discovered a man who knows a whole lot about a lot. A fountain of incredible knowledge. He can communicate ideas and experiences in exciting and adventurous ways. His observation of facts ignites my imagination, and any time spent with him is most enjoyable, leaving me wondering when I will see him again. "Kind" is the most underwhelming word to describe him, but he would prefer you not embellish. That is the type of man he is. Peter has instilled wonderful moral values in me. "Stay humble" is the one I value most. For all of this, your generosity and guidance, and to call you my friend, I thank you.

To Dr. Muni Mysore: She was the voice of reason and reality once a month, every month, for twenty-seven years. She was my sanity when I thought I'd surely lost it. She found my balance when I couldn't stop stumbling. She was the one I finally believed when she said, "Everything is going to be okay."

I recall sitting in her waiting room one afternoon, for a session on depression, when the woman next to me confided that her cat had just committed suicide. Suddenly, things didn't seem so bad. Yes, everything was going to be okay. She is an extraordinary psychiatrist and a wonderful human being. I consider myself extremely fortunate and am very grateful to have had her treat me all those years. I hope you are enjoying your retirement. I thank you very much.

To Solmaz Nafez: This fine lady sets an example, every single day of her life, of how to treat another human being with kindness and respect. There is never any doubt that she is sincere in her actions and words. You can trust her completely. You can depend on her absolutely. I should strive to be like her, and if I ever succeeded, I would still only be half the human being she is. I am grateful for her care. For this and so much more, I thank you.

To Doris Klassen: I could write another book just about you. It would be a self-help book filled with "Doris-isms." I must have written a hundred of them down and read them a thousand times. I will simply say ... she was my best friend. She took me to places and events I'd never been. She taught me to brave the world. How to survive in it. How to thrive in it. And to "always have something to look forward to." This was her mantra for fighting depression. It is now mine. She is on another journey now. I miss you. I love you. And I thank you. **And to your grandson Scott:** You were very helpful with valuable information that I used in the book. For your kindness and for your service, I thank you.

To Dennis & Joan Walker: You don't have to see each other every day to call each other friends. You are loving, kind, generous, and silly, bringing joy to everyone who knows you and comfort to so many who need it. Dennis, without you, I would have no computer, cell phone, plumbing, or lighting! Thank goodness your wife is so giving of your time! Joan, you taught me a craft that calms my nerves and makes me feel accomplished. Your cooking is second to none. The two of you have helped me greatly. For this, I thank you both.

To Mike Altham: For letting me interview you more than once. You were patient and thorough. Although this is a book of fiction, the integrity of facts included in it were very important to me. You provided that. Your background and experience are invaluable. You have been to the war and back, and you were triumphant. You are brave and humble, a wealth of knowledge, and a gracious human being. For your incredible kindness and your service, I thank you.

To Dr. Frank Renouf: You were my first chosen family physician, and the following things meant so much to me in my early twenties when I was struggling horrendously: For asking me to always book the last appointment of the day, as you wanted to take the time needed for me to be heard, and for us to talk about an action plan for success regarding my "physical, mental, and emotional well-being." For eventually referring me to Dr. Mysore. For all the years you never gave up on me, I will remember you as "the best." I hope you are enjoying your retirement. For everything you've accomplished, for all that you did for me, I thank you.

To Dr. Johann Raubenheimer, a superb doctor with a gentle nature, thorough and proactive: For taking me on as a patient when you had so many. For <u>always</u> listening and treating me with kindness. For helping me to get a proper diagnosis of the debilitating affliction called fibromyalgia. I had never heard of it before. Its disabling nature greatly changed the quality of my life. Many doctors don't really believe in it, but you did, and you've helped me greatly. It has been many years now. For closely monitoring it and aggressively treating me, I thank you.

To Kelly Bond: The impressive one-on-one experience of your interview was very valuable to me, both as excellent research for this book and in helping me to realize just how important and dangerous your occupation really is. The appreciation I gained for police departments as a whole was truly overwhelming. Your smile and the way you regaled me with stories sparked my imagination. All of this was of great benefit to me. Your handshake was welcoming yet guarded. It made me wonder if you are ever off duty. I have decided you are not. I felt safe around you, Kelly. For your time, and for your service, I thank you.

To Wajih "G" Zeid: When I was having trouble expanding my inner circle, your warm eyes and soft voice helped me drop my guard. My anxiety lessened. You had a smile for me every time I saw you, and you consistently asked me how I was. He cares about his business, and he cares about his family most of all. G shares openly. I will always call him my friend, and I thank him.

To Malcom Bell: Your accomplishments are incredible. As we sat in that restaurant on that rainy night, you provided the most candid interview I have ever done. You opened my eyes and my heart. I will never forget it. Your knowledge, experience, and gentleness pave the way for others. I am grateful to know you, call you my friend, and I thank you.

To Dr. Christopher Bourque, my former neurologist: You are a gentleman and a "gentle man," one who after every appointment would say to me, "Keep fighting the good fight." It was an encouraging thing to say, always made me smile, and I share it with others. I miss your dry sense of humor, as do most of your patients, I'm sure. I hope you are enjoying your retirement. For all that you did for me, I thank you.

To Wes Schilke, my dear brother: I just know you are smiling. I have paid tribute to you so many times in this book. I hope I made you laugh. I hope your journey is incredible and that your "sweetheart" is at your side. For all the times you let me play with my dolls while you played pool with your friends and listened to The Beatles. You never once shooed me away. I knew most of their songs by the time I was six. For all the early

Saturday mornings when you watched Bugs Bunny with me and laughed yourself sick every single time Wile E. Coyote got hit with an anvil. For taking me dancing when I was eighteen but threatening to beat up anyone who asked me to dance. What a guy you were. What a life you lived. I miss you everyday. For loving me, and for being you, I thank you.

To Calvin Schilke: *"Hey, Cal! Did I tell you I love you today? Cause I love you."* My sweet brother. For the candid interview you gave. I appreciate the vast knowledge you shared. For all your unbelievable true-life stories. You could write your own book, and you should. For all the wonderful camping and fishing trips you've taken me on, and the memories to last a lifetime. Thank you for the gray jays that landed on my hand, the friendly moose, and the wolf that looked me in the eyes. For the serenity, healing, bust-a-gut fun, and the peace of mother nature that you provided for writing. And for literally saving my life. For loving me, for being you, I thank you.

To Rosa Giampaolo: Ever have someone you can confide anything to? That's Rosa. She is a great friend. Rosa cares about you and her work ethic. She truly wants you to be happy and shows you by her actions every day. I have known her for some time, and we get along like peas and carrots. There's a lot of laughter in our friendship, and I'm grateful for that. We share our hopes and dreams, our love of family, and daily events. She has been a big cheerleader of mine for as long as I've known her. For all these reasons, I thank you.

To Gordon Stanger: I call him "Gordly," a best friend indeed. We labeled ourselves ABFFs years ago, for laughs, and it stuck. A kind-hearted, gentle man, who always puts others before himself. So many people love him for his outgoing personality and contagious smile. I love him. We have spent hours and hours laughing together. Especially enjoying our movie nights. He has taken me on incredible adventures and will be in my life forever. It has to be said just how much Gord takes care of me. He often drives me to appointments and we have fun shopping together. If I am not well, he makes sure I have a hand to hold to keep me steady. More than a great friend, he is family. If not for Gord's incredible kindness, this novel may never have been published. For all of this, I thank you.

To Terry & Donny White: For your unconditional love and support. For all the fun and laughter (our trip to Minneapolis comes to mind). Terry's giggles and Donny's stories. The endless phone calls and guidance. To be able to call you my friends. For all of this and more, I thank you both.

To extended family and friends: To all the other people in my life that I have been fortunate enough to know and call my friends, I thank you. To the immediate family on my husband's side, I would like to say this: The difficult tasks I deal with on a daily basis can be challenging. It's very painful to explain, but I do the very best I can. I will never give up fighting. Encouragement, positivity, and kindness is the motto of your family, and I have benefitted greatly. I deeply thank my husband's family for all their support over the years, with a tremendous amount of gratitude going to Eleanor and Cy Galloway for being excellent role models for me in my early twenties. To everyone, for everything, I thank you.

To my readers: Try not to consider yourself someone who "suffers from" whatever ails you but rather someone who "lives with" whatever it is that challenges you. We are all imperfect human beings. To be accepted as such is the greatest respect one can receive. This book has been a long labor of love—*love for myself*. I hope you found it somewhat entertaining, and perhaps a little helpful as well. For your time and understanding, I thank you.

Printed in the USA
CPSIA information can be obtained
at www.ICGtesting.com
JSHW020932091224
74935JS00002B/6